D1164075

PEL AND THE
PROMISED LAND

PEL AND THE
PROMISED LAND

Mark Hebden

St. Martin's Press
New York

Library of Congress Cataloging-in-Publication Data
Hebden, Mark
Pel and the promised land / Mark Hebden.
p.   cm.
"A Thomas Dunne book."
ISBN 0-312-08872-8
I. Title.
PR6058.A6886P466   1993
823'.914—dc20   92-36539   CIP

First Published in Great Britain by
Constable & Company Ltd.

First U.S. Edition: January 1993
10 9 8 7 6 5 4 3 2 1

Though readers may decide they have recognized the city in these pages, in fact it is intended to be fictitious.

PEL AND THE
PROMISED LAND

1

It was late in the afternoon and Chief Inspector Evariste Clovis Désiré Pel was feeling low as he stared morosely at his blotter. It has just occurred to him that he was twenty-four hours older than he had been at the same time the previous day. It was a fact that took the breath away. There were only 8760 hours in a year, so that, given thirty more years of life, he had only 262800 hours left to live. It wasn't long and all he had achieved in his years of toil, he felt, was to become an official in the province of Burgundy of the Brigade Criminelle of the Police Judiciaire of the Republic of France. And one who had passed his prime into the bargain.

It wasn't true, of course. There was a lot left in Pel. He would have felt cheated if there hadn't been. But the mood was far from unusual. Pel was never a man to look on the bright side.

In fact, he realized, when you thought about it, things were even worse than he had contemplated. Those hours he had so carefully calculated gave him only 15768000 minutes and 15768000 minutes added up to only 946080000 seconds. And, name of God, he thought, a second wasn't very long. No more than a second.

What was more, he had a cold coming on, so he probably wouldn't last even that long. The germs were waiting for him everywhere, ugly, menacing, fanged and hairy, always ready to pull him down.

Pel was trying hard to live up to his reputation. Gloom was one of his few pleasures. But it was always harder to be bad-tempered in the sort of weather they were having at the moment. In addition, he was comfortably married after expecting never to be wanted by anyone, and was carefully nurtured by a woman who seemed happy to accept him, warts and all, without complaint.

Being depressed grew harder every day. Even the Society of Bigots, of which he was president, secretary and only member, didn't occupy a lot of his time these days, because on the whole he had remarkably little to complain about. He could well imagine a miserable old age unable to avoid being happy.

He lit a cigarette. He had tried on many occasions to give them up — millions did; why couldn't he? — but had finally come to realize he would never ever manage it. As he drew a luxurious lungful of smoke down to his socks, he reflected that they were bound to kill him off before long with asthma, cancer or one of the associated diseases. Everybody said so.

'I almost cracked it once,' he pointed out. 'I went two days without one. Do you think I'm likely to die before my allotted span?'

Detective Inspector Daniel Darcy looked up from the other side of the desk. He was smoking, too. But Darcy was in good spirits and looked at the peak of his form. His teeth shone like the jewels in a Disney cartoon and his profile seemed highly polished and in top gear.

'I might just as well slash my wrists,' Pel ended gloomily.

Darcy grinned. 'Why not have your lungs replaced by an electric pump?' he suggested. 'It would involve a big operation, mind you.'

Pel gave his deputy a sour look. He didn't appreciate humour so late in the day — especially when he was on the receiving end. It wasn't, he considered bitterly, just that Darcy seemed to feel assured of living longer; it was simply that he didn't appear to give a damn.

Pel had been in a resentful mood all day. He had just completed one of the fatuous forms which occasionally appeared in the pipeline, demanding the answers to questions which some half-witted government jack-in-office insisted would enable the department to handle crime with greater efficiency. There were sheets of them, ending up with a request for personal data which was not only a waste of time but downright impertinent. Where were you born? And why? Full address. Full name. *That* always irritated Pel because he was the child of an ambitious woman who had seen her son as a future president of the Republic and had given him the names to go with the position. Evariste, Clovis and Désiré were enough to make a man worry rats. They had been the cause of considerable aggression in the school playground and a great deal of laughter among the girls who had been curious enough to ask what he was called. One had actually fallen out of bed laughing. What was worse, she hadn't bothered to climb back in.

In addition to all this weight he had to carry, he had an extra temporary source of bitterness because his wife was on one of her occasional trips to Paris and he was at the mercy of their housekeeper, Madame Routy. Madame Pel ran a hairdressing establishment in the Rue de la Liberté which was rapidly becoming famous — if only for the prices that were charged. To the boutique she had opened next door in case her clients had anything left after they'd settled up, had been added a children's wear establishment, a sportswear shop, a teenagers' shop and a shop that sold nothing but denim. She seemed to Pel to be raking in money hand over fist. Not that Pel minded. He was all for anything that would make his old age more comfortable. Police pensions never led to a life of debauched luxury and it relieved him of the terror of ultimate penury.

The only snag was that Madame Pel, being a good business woman, occasionally had to attend to the sticks and stones of her livelihood and disappear into the blue to attend to financial and other matters. And when she did, Pel felt bereft, orphaned from the moment she walked out of the door.

He shifted a few papers round on his desk and looked at Darcy. Darcy had been in court all day and was only just delivering his daily résumé of what they had in hand.

'*Alors,*' Pel said heavily. 'Inform me.'

Darcy, who had known Pel a long time and had a shrewd idea what was going on at the back of his mind, smiled to himself.

'Misset's made an ass of himself again, *patron,*' he said.

'That's nothing new.' Misset was Pel's *bête noire,* the only member of his team who didn't pull his weight. He had been in danger on many occasions of being returned to the uniformed branch but had regularly defeated the attempts by unexpectedly pulling off something spectacular.

'What was it this time?' Pel asked.

'That stabbing in the Rue Frères Lumières. Nothing much in itself, but he got the names the wrong way round. The magistrates found they were trying the victim.'

'One day,' Pel said darkly, 'Misset will cut his own throat.'

'I doubt if he's that competent.'

'What else?'

'Everybody else's busy. Do you want the details?'

'Not if everybody's busy. I like to see them busy. It prevents mutiny. What about Nosjean and De Troq'?'

Darcy shrugged. Known as the Heavenly Twins, Sergeants Jean-Luc Nosjean and Charles-Victor de Troquereau needed no supervision. They worked together excellently, were young, bright and energetic, and could be trusted.

'That garage at Genois that was broken into. They think the owner's been handling hot cars and that somebody was trying to identify something that belonged to him. The course of the enquiry seems to have changed direction. I gather they're due to wind it up any day now. I think it'll be the owner they'll pull in, not the type who broke in.'

'Go on.'

'There's a request from the police at Evian. There's been a spate of smuggling down there and they've asked us to keep our eyes open.'

Pel's features rearranged themselves to register disapproval. Switzerland intruded into his territory at Pontarlier and just to the south round Geneva on Lac Léman, which the Swiss, with a chauvinism to match anything the French could produce, had the cheek to refer to as Lake Geneva. From time to time they called on each other for assistance. At others, their interests clashed and there were eyeball-to-eyeball confrontations.

Pel was French enough to imagine there was nothing anybody in France, let alone Burgundy, could ever want from anywhere else. 'What would we need to smuggle from Switzerland?' he demanded. 'The secret of the cuckoo clock?'

Darcy grinned. 'Insides of watches. The Swiss are complaining.'

'They always do.'

'There's somebody getting them across the lake. If anything crops up, we've been asked to pass it on. I don't suppose there will be. The rest of the boys are involved with the usual. A complaint's come in from Rogeaux-sur-Ile. Type called Barthelot. Says someone's poisoning his sheep. Brochard says he'll deal with it.'

Pel was suspicious at once. Cops didn't usually volunteer for things without good reason. 'Where's Brochard now?'

'Next door.'

'Have him in.'

Brochard was young and looked far more naïve than he was. They often used him on cases where there was a woman involved. He looked as if he needed mothering, and it was surprising what he found out just by looking innocent.

'Why do you want to handle this sheep poisoning?' Pel asked.

'I know about sheep,' Brochard pointed out. 'My father's a farmer. He has sheep.'

'And you think you can handle it?'

'Easy, *patron*. I bet it's a fiddle. I know those farmers up there in Rogeaux. They're as cunning as a lot of weasels. I bet this Barthelot's up to something. Or else he's plain stupid. I know all the tricks, and what I don't know my Old Man does.'

'And doubtless you'll want a day or two off to seek his advice?'

Brochard grinned. 'It would help, *patron*.'

As Brochard left, Pel looked at Darcy. 'That young man's sometimes too bright for his own good,' he observed darkly. 'What else?'

Darcy flipped through his files again. 'Lagé's on that fiddle at St-Pol,' he said. 'It's complicated. It'll take a long time.'

'That'll suit Lagé. He goes slowly but he's thorough. The more detailed it is the better he likes it. What about that rumour that the forest fire at St-Etois was started deliberately?'

'Chief Lapeur of the Sapeurs Pompiers thinks it was. But he's got no proof. He put his experts on it. All they learned was that there was a gale blowing and it swept away twenty-five hectares of woodland in one night.'

'Why does the Fire Chief think it might have been deliberate?'

'It's happened before, *patron*. That house in the Rue de la Poésie. Chief Lapeur thinks that was another. He says it had all the signs. Indications of a fierce core of flame where there was no reason for fierce flames. He won't be definite but he suspects kerosene or petrol. He wondered if the owners set it on fire for the insurance. We're checking. Aimedieu's handling it.'

Pel nodded. Aimedieu was young but he was reliable. 'Does it have much land?'

'Quite a bit. Around a hectare.'

Pel stared intently at his blotter for a moment. Darcy frowned.

'The land wasn't destroyed,' he said. 'Except by firemen with feet like camels trampling everything flat. Why, *patron*? Is it important?'

'It's worth bearing in mind,' Pel pointed out. 'We've had a routine report from Paris on these unexplained blazes where land's involved, and a request to keep our eyes open.'

'What's behind it, *patron*?'

'Speculators are believed to be starting fires. They pick on restricted land, destroy it, then slap in a request for building permission on the grounds that it's become waste land. And they're getting it, too. After a place's been devastated by fire, no one can object that it's a beauty spot. They then put in an application and shove up a complex of buildings and, *hé op*, before you know where you are, what was a bosky dell has become a small select housing estate on the fringe of the country with excellent outlook, good accessibility and all mod. cons. Someone must be getting a rake off.'

'It's happened before, *patron*,' Darcy said drily. 'And, with the housing law as it is and the need for homes everywhere, it leaves itself wide open to the fly boys. It all comes back to the same thing in the end. The environment. It's getting crowded.'

Brochard had left the office delighted with himself. He hadn't expected Pel to give way so easily and a little of his mother's cooking would go down well.

He decided to celebrate with a drink and chose the Bar du Destin. It was a dark little place full of pot plants you could hide behind. Pel had once been in the habit of going there to brood. Last time in there Brochard had spotted a girl and she might be in there again. Brochard was in need of a girl-friend. He was good-looking enough to have a lot of girl-friends and he had just broken off with the latest, who lived in Talant. Not without tears, bad temper and threats, mind you, so it had seemed a good idea at the time to find a bar a long way from where she lived.

'I'll shame you,' she had stormed. 'I'll take an overdose of sleeping pills just to show you up!'

Collecting his beer, Brochard had looked for a table. At one of them, two youngsters had been clutching each other, the boy's hand on the girl's thigh, their mouths clamped together as if they'd been welded. Dark bars were always the haunts of lovers and lost souls. The only available table had been occupied by a solitary girl drinking coffee — the one he was looking for now. She was pretty and had long legs and didn't seem to mind showing them. She had been studying a sketch book of drawings.

'Mind if I sit here?' Brochard had said.

She had moved her seat a little and removed her handbag from the table. It was as big as a portmanteau and most of its contents were spread across the table. She had begun to collect them up and stuff them inside. The pile of coins seemed big enough to start a bank with.

'Isn't it heavy?' Brochard had asked.

She had grinned at him and they had begun to talk. She was a book illustrator, she had said. 'What do *you* do?'

'Enquiries,' Brochard had answered cautiously. Being a cop sometimes put a girl off.

'What sort of enquiries?'

'Insurance.'

Her name was Carlota Ciasca — Charlie for short — and she came from the Jura. He suspected there was a bit of Italian in there somewhere. She was dark, the name was right and it wasn't unusual. The Italians had been moving north for generations looking for summer jobs around the

Swiss lakes, and a few had spilled over into other places, married Swiss or French, and settled down.

It had turned out that his guess was a good one. Papa Ciasca's family had originally come from the Italian side of Lake Lugano. Papa Ciasca now spent his time making gifts for tourists. He painted and framed the sort of pictures that were repeated *ad nauseam* at every resort along the European lakes, and assembled cuckoo clocks and musical boxes from ready-carved pieces bought in bulk from Brienz, Engadine and Berne.

It hadn't taken long for Brochard to suggest to the girl that they should meet again. Why not, he had thought. Having just got rid of one girl, he had virtually walked into the arms of another.

Because he had no wish to go home to a house devoid of wife and comfort, Pel worked late. He liked working late. It gave him more things to worry about and a good reason to complain to the Chief that he was being put upon.

As he left, he bumped into the Chief himself. The Chief eyed him warily. He was a big man who had been noted as a boxer in his youth. In his period in uniform he had settled disputes with clouts round the head rather than hauling off a wrongdoer to the Hôtel de Police for an appearance before the magistrates. There were many who considered it an excellent idea, because it saved the gaols from becoming overcrowded, the magistrates from complaining, the individual cop from a lot of paperwork, and the wrongdoer from a lot of wasted time in a cell.

'You're late,' he said to Pel.

'Work,' Pel explained, laying it on.

'Come into my office. I'd like a word.'

A whisky bottle appeared and the Chief poured out two good doses. *'Santé,'* he said.

Pel eyed him uneasily. Something was in the wind, he

15

knew. The whisky didn't appear for anything unimportant.

'Know that farm at Tar-le-Petit?' the Chief asked. 'The farmer died and his wife moved into a cottage in the village. It's right alongside the road. I saw it the other night. It's a wreck.'

'So I heard. Who owns it?'

'I heard it was bought by a type called Feray — Lucien Feray. it was an attractive place. Not a lot of land, but enough. Nice view at the back over the valley. I was having dinner up that way the other evening and heard Feray put in an application to pull it down. He wanted to build an estate of twenty *de luxe* executive dwellings.'

'I heard that, too.'

'The application was refused on the grounds that it was of historical interest. Eighteenth-century outbuildings or something. So Feray rented it to a type called Denis Clos. He then put in an application to turn it into a night-club. That was slapped down as fast as the other. So he and Clos turned it into a kennels.'

'And?'

'That project went bust. The rumour up there is that Clos hadn't any money, anyway, and that he was nothing but the front for Feray and that Feray was in with someone else who was interested in the place. When Clos left, Feray closed the place up but vandals got in and wrecked it. So it can hardly be called of historic interest now, can it? The windows have corrugated iron sheeting nailed over them. The door's boarded up. The roof's falling in. The outbuildings caught fire and half of them went.' The Chief refilled Pel's glass. 'The rumour up there now is that Feray was working with Clos. They've both got records. I took the trouble to have them looked up. The story is that Feray *allowed* the vandals in. Deliberately. Even *sent* them in.'

Pel shrugged. 'So they can put in an application to pull it down and build the original set of detached executive dwellings. I was talking to Darcy about this very thing. The

Sapeurs Pompiers think that forest fire at St-Etois might have been deliberate – for the same reason. The owners knew they'd never get permission to build there, so they destroyed it. Now they'll sit on it for two or three years and try again before it's had time to recover.'

The Chief nodded. 'I've just come from Paris,' he said. 'The Minister for the Environment's concerned. He's planning legislation to thwart the property speculators. It's almost a plague along the Mediterranean coast. Arsonists are *known* to be involved. They're trying to draft a law to ban the development of fire-ravaged land for fifteen years to stop people building holiday homes for foreign buyers. After all, land's profitable these days. Imagine sitting on a few hectares of beauty spot that brings nothing in. If it ceases to be a beauty spot and someone buys it for development, you could become very wealthy. The Minister's ordered a census of all land burned in the last ten years to see what's become of it. Most of the new developments in the Bouches du Rhône area near Marseilles have been on burnt-out land. *And* in Var and round St-Trop'. Too many people have started playing golf and there's too much demand for new courses.'

'It's a pity people can't stick to the old games like boules,' Pel said.

The Chief grinned. 'There are over fifty applications for new courses in that area,' he said. 'With them, of course, come applications for new housing, because people like to live near their leisure. Houses are followed by supermarkets, garages, restaurants, shopping precincts. A fifteen-year ban would give the forests time to recover. The aim's to stop the shady developers with the money. Stop *them* and we'll probably stop the fire-raisers. Let's keep an eye on it, shall we?'

'The fire-raisers?'

'Vandals would do,' the Chief snapped. 'We have them. At Tar-le-Petit. And, if you're interested, there are three separate applications in the office of the Department of the Environment for new golf courses in our area. One near Tar-le-Petit.'

Pel was frowning as he arrived home. The evening was magnificent. As his car had climbed from the city he could see across the whole sun-bright Plateau de Langres, dramatic against a sky dark with thunderclouds. This, he thought, was Burgundy. Not the tourists' paradise, the wine tastings round the vineyards, the old chateaux — but the countryside, to true Burgundians like himself the promised land.

Madame Routy, the housekeeper, he decided as he entered the house, would be watching television. Pel and Madame Routy had been enjoying a mutual enmity for more years than either of them cared to remember. She had been his housekeeper before his marriage, and his wife — perhaps realizing their need for the adrenalin their dislike stirred up — had taken on Madame Routy with Pel. She had been tamed a little, of course, since then, and only broke out of confinement nowadays when Madame disappeared on one of her business trips. With Madame at home, the house ran on oiled wheels, with fresh flowers and meals of unbelievable splendour. With Madame away, the flowers wilted. There were stale croissants for breakfast and the coffee tasted like shellac, while the evening meal invariably consisted of one of the overcooked and shrivelled casseroles Madame Routy had daily presented him before his marriage.

The television would be turned up to full volume so that it sounded like a rocket blasting off, and she would be sitting in the *confort anglais*, the best chair in the house, doubtless with a nip of Pel's whisky in her hand. None of these things did she dare when Madame was about. But when Madame was away, she obviously considered it important to regain all the ground she had lost when she had surrendered authority.

Her eyes icy, she had handed Pel his brief case that morning as if she hoped it contained a bomb. He had heard the television go on, turned up beyond 'Loud' to 'Shattering' before he had driven out of the drive. Even Yves Pasquier, the small boy from next door, on his way to school, seemed to wince at the sound, while his dog had turned back to the house with its tail between its legs.

As he had expected, Madame Routy *was* watching television, and not on the small set in her room at the back of the house, but on the big set in the salon that Pel's wife enjoyed. She was, as Pel had suspected she would be, sitting in the *confort anglais*. There was a whiff of whisky in the air and when Pel went to pour himself a tot, he noticed it had gone down in the bottle. Being on the mean side – careful, he preferred to call it – he always made a point of noticing where the level was against the lettering on the label. This time it came to 'Bottled in Scotland' instead of '100% Scotch Whiskies', which was where Pel had left it the night before.

'It's a fashion programme,' Madame Routy explained over her shoulder without taking her eyes off the screen for a second. 'You can see better on the big set. I didn't think Madame would mind.'

Madame, Pel felt, would willingly have offered Madame Routy a view of the fashions while she was watching herself, but she certainly wouldn't have encouraged it without. But he muttered something about having a headache and slunk off to his study, asking himself for the hundredth time why he didn't tip up the *confort anglais* and deposit Madame Routy on the floor with a roar of 'You've been at the whisky again!'

He sighed, wondering why he, who had faced men with clubs and guns, could never find the courage to put Madame Routy in her place. His life before his marriage had been a misery of discomfort and noise. Then an expression of sly malice crossed his face. He would let Madame Routy prepare and cook one of her poisonous dishes and at the last moment say he had to go out and would have to eat in the city, so that she would have to polish off her repulsive concoction herself. It was a ploy he had used on numerous occasions and it always gave him great pleasure.

At just about the time Pel was enjoying the disgusted expression on Madame Routy's face at his announcement, at Vieilles Etuves to the south, a young man called Robert Flandres was manoeuvring his car among the trees of the Forêt de Diviot.

He was a smart young man with the sort of profile and teeth Darcy had but, somehow, without the honesty that shone out of Darcy's face like a searchlight. The girl with him was not his wife. She was his secretary and, like Pel, they had been working late.

It was a fine night and the thunderclouds Pel had seen had passed. They had eaten well and drunk a little too much and the young man was a smooth worker. After a little heavy breathing in the back of the car, he opened the door.

'It's a bit cramped in here,' he said. 'Let's get out. It's warm enough.'

The girl climbed out and sniffed the air. There was a subtle end-of-summer smell. There had been a little rain recently and the forest had the musty smell of decaying vegetable matter, even though the leaves were still on the trees. It was just growing dark and the woods seemed grey and faintly menacing.

'We're a long way from anywhere,' she said nervously.

She knew why she'd been brought there and was not unwilling, but somehow she wasn't very happy either. She could smell wood smoke — probably from Vieilles Etuves, the small village on the side of the hill that they'd passed five minutes before. There was a loud crack near by and she jumped.

'Tree,' Flandres said, putting his arms round her and kissing her. 'They expand in the heat or something.'

For a while they stood together, Flandres's hand feeling for the edge of the girl's skirt. He had thought of everything and produced a thick car rug which he spread on the grass alongside a sheltering hedge of undergrowth. The girl was not exactly starry-eyed and bursting with romance and as she sat down on the rug and the young man joined her, she flapped her hand.

'Flies,' she commented.

'It's the heat.'

She stared suspiciously at the darkening foliage alongside her and sniffed. 'There's somebody here,' she whispered.

Flandres reached for her. 'You can smell them?'

'I can feel it.'

'Can't be.'

She wasn't satisfied and continued to stare about her. Then she gave a nervous little giggle and pointed. 'That's what got me going,' she said. 'I knew there was something. Someone's lost a shoe.'

Among the undergrowth she could see a lavender-coloured high-heeled shoe marked with a smear of yellowish mud.

'I bet she was up to something to leave her shoe behind,' she remarked.

'When you've got a girl going at full revs,' Flandres observed cheerfully,' she doesn't always know what she's doing.'

She gave another giggle and put out a hand to move the shoe away. As she pushed at it, her eyes widened. The young man failed to notice. As he reached lustfully for her again she shoved an elbow sharp as a dagger in his chest. He pushed her down on to the rug, but she struggled free, panting and scared. Brushing her hands aside, he grabbed her again, but she swung her arm back to land a clout at the side of his head that rattled his teeth.

'What's that for?'

She was still staring beyond him at the shoe. While he was still rubbing his cheek, she pushed again at it. It didn't move and she let out a full-blooded scream right in the young man's ear.

'Name of God,' she yelled. 'It's got a foot in it!'

2

When Pel looked into woodland fires over the past five years, he found there had been ten cases in the countryside around, which Chief Lapeur of the Fire Service considered might have been started deliberately. In three cases, it had been found that insurance was the reason and three men had been sent to prison for destroying their own property. That left seven and in three instances it seemed to be a case of protest by villagers against foreign interlopers. The worst case was a three-million-franc luxury home at Lermes-et-Chênes, destroyed when on the point of completion by what appeared to be a home-made bomb. Though nobody was prepared to admit guilt, noticeably nobody had expressed regret, especially when it had been announced that plans to build two other houses had fallen through.

It seemed a good idea to see Judge Castéou, who had been handed the case. Ghislaine Castéou was petite and pretty and was standing in for Judge Polverari who was off sick.

Immediately they found themselves on the subject of foreign buyers. It seemed to crop up every time any two people met together.

'Of course it's foreigners,' Judge Castéou observed. 'Not them personally, but they're behind it all. There are hundreds of British buying homes in France.'

'I can't imagine hundreds of French buying homes in

Britain,' Pel said.

Judge Castéou laughed. 'I have relations in the Dordogne,' she pointed out. 'The foreigners were just a trickle when they went there. Now they're a flood. Between thirty and forty houses a day are being sold to British buyers. Even the British who live there are getting worried it's all going wrong. They're beginning now to think they're going to have Costa del Sol developments because they're getting people now who aren't buying because they love the Dordogne, but because they've decided it's a good investment.'

'The Chief,' Pel pointed out in a doom-laden voice, 'has it that now they've exhausted the Dordogne and the South they're moving into Burgundy.'

It was decided it might be a good idea to pick up Denis Clos and Lucien Feray. The vandalism at Tar-le-Petit seemed to have potentialities, and a few questions in the right quarter seemed to be in order.

'Feray's a big guy,' Darcy said. 'His record's mostly for bodily harm. I can well imagine him being used for that sort of thing. I'll get Misset to find out where he's got to.'

'It might be one way of getting rid of Misset,' Pel said.

Misset answered Darcy's summons nervously. He was well aware that he was once more in danger of being returned to uniform.

'Just be careful,' Darcy warned him. 'Feray could react.'

'I know,' Misset said. 'I once had to haul him in for assault.'

'What happened?'

'He handed me a black eye.'

Darcy gave Misset a sour look. 'Not you! Him!'

'Oh! He was sent down for two months. It would have been three but he told the magistrates that as I was in plain clothes he didn't think I was a cop.'

Sometimes Darcy didn't think so either.

'I owe him one,' Misset went on.

24

'Well, forget it,' Darcy snapped. 'Don't get involved. We want to know what's going on, not how hard he punches. Find out where he is and who his friends are. When we want him we can take the whole department along if necessary. Even a few tanks and paratroopers. Just turn up where he is and whom he's talking to. We'll do the rest.'

They had just started things moving when, two days later, the morning produced the sort of sunshine you can only find in Burgundy, with blue sky dotted with puffballs of cloud. The weather had pulled out all the stops and in the glittering morning air the city had a look of festivity about it that came solely from the golden glow on the front of the buildings and the varnished tiles of the roofs round the Church of Notre Dame. Even the traffic seemed more sedate than usual.

About ten forty-five a large dark blue van that looked as though it belonged to a security concern cruised along the Boulevard Maréchal Joffre, its two occupants wearing crash helmets and what looked like uniforms. It pulled into a vacant space by the kerb and the men inside began to watch the clock on the dashboard. At almost the same time, a grey Citroën pulled into a vacant space some distance behind. There was nothing unusual about either vehicle except that the van was parked outside a bank and the Citroën outside Merciers', a jeweller's which catered for affluent customers from the best end of the city.

The street was wide and, being part of a one-way system, should have had a free flow of traffic. But at that time of the day near the bank there was always a little congestion although opposite Merciers', off to the right, was another wide street, the Rue Albert Premier, and because there was no traffic in the opposite direction, it was easy to turn into. The road system had been devised to take traffic away from the banking area, but there was one disadvantage which

25

hadn't occurred to the planners but had been noticed and passed on to the man in the front passenger seat of the Citroën. His name was Jean-Pierre Orega and, as he watched what was happening further along the street, he decided everything was going according to instructions.

It pleased him to tell his associates that the idea was his. In fact, it wasn't. He had been told to get on with it, and only the details had been worked out in the shabby house in the Rue St. Josephe, in the Arsenal area of the city, that he called his headquarters.

Orega wasn't a clever man and because of that hadn't ever managed to stay out of prison long. He still considered himself big time, however, and never wasted much of his life after being given his freedom before he started planning something else. As a result he was regularly returned to 72, Rue d'Auxonne, by which unobtrusive name was known the city's gaol.

He fished out a Gauloise and stuck it between his lips. His eyes narrowed behind the wrap-around dark glasses he liked to affect. He wore them because he felt they hid his identity and gave him a look of menace. Considering himself a big wheel, he liked to dress and behave with the image, with sharp clothes and, when he could find them, smart wisecracks to go with them. Nothing pleased him more than when he was called on by bigger wheels than he was to perform some *coup* for them, as was happening at that moment.

'You ready?' he asked the driver alongside him.

A grunt informed him the driver was prepared.

'The cop's there,' Orega said, indicating a policeman on traffic duty near the van further down the road. 'When they move, the cop's going to go for *them*. They've been making themselves look suspicious and he's watching them. And when he does go for them, that's when *I* move. By the time he finds they're doing no harm we'll be gone. *Ça va?*'

'OK.'

Jean-Pierre Orega tossed his cigarette through the window of the Citroën with a flourish, took off his glasses and patted his inside pocket for the reassuring feel of the Smith and Wesson five shot .38 that reposed there.

'Just coming up to time,' he said. 'Stand by.'

As though at a signal, a puff of smoke came from the exhaust of the dark van down the road, and from the Citroën they saw a sudden surge of activity. People began to scatter and the policeman began to run.

'Now!' Jean-Pierre Orega dived from the car and into the jeweller's. Within a minute he was back with two trays of rings.

'Get going!' he shouted and the car accelerated, flinging Orega back in the seat. The policeman down the street, who was just turning away from the van, saw the Citroën roar into the Rue Albert Premier and the jeweller's assistants hurtle into the street screaming blue murder. He had gone for the wrong target. The van had turned out to be empty and, despite the suspicious behaviour of its crew, was apparently innocent of any crime.

All might have been well if only Jean-Pierre Orega had been as clever as he thought he was. But, because he had felt the police might be keeping a watch on the house he so grandiloquently called his headquarters, he had used the Parc de la Columbière to sort out the instructions for the hold-up. He ought to have known that five hard-faced men sitting in a circle on the little white-painted iron chairs in the park, gesturing and arguing in undertones, would attract attention.

And so it had.

Sergeants Nosjean and De Troquereau, sitting in a car watching the park for the man they believed to have been involved in the hot car deals at Genois, had noticed them at once. They had been discussing Claudie Darel, the only female member of Pel's team. At one time both of them had pursued her, with De Troq', being a baron, always slightly in the lead. As they talked, they noticed the five men on the chairs synchronizing watches and apparently making plans.

'Looks interesting,' Nosjean observed.

When the men split up, the two policemen casually made a note of the numbers of the cars they used to drive away — just in case.

With the result that as soon as the information on the hold-up came through, Nosjean radioed the Hôtel de Police and Jean-Pierre Ortega and three of his friends, traced at once through their cars, were brought in within two hours.

Pel and Darcy had just returned from the Chief's conference when Nosjean and De Troq' appeared, grinning all over their faces. They hadn't bothered to call out the troops. They had called for assistance from Morell and Debray, who were in another car near by, and made the arrests themselves, turning up at the Rue St. Josephe while Inspector Turgot of Uniformed Branch, assisted by Detective Officer Aimedieu, Inspector Pomereu of Traffic, and a cloud of odds and ends were still arriving outside Merciers'.

Jean-Pierre Orega and his friends were already in the cells awaiting attention before the Hôtel de Police had properly digested the news of the robbery. They hadn't even begun to divide up the loot. They had still been sitting around toasting their success, and couldn't understand how the police had got on to them so quickly.

'It's an old dodge,' Darcy said after congratulations had been handed round to all and sundry. 'Draw the police attention away with a perfectly innocent vehicle and, while their eyes are on that, send in another one to do the job. It might have worked, too, but for Nosjean and De Troq'.' He consulted the file in his hand. 'Names: Jean-Pierre Orega. Calls himself a director. God knows what of. André

Duchesne, van driver. Philippe Kerjean, bricklayer. Robert Bola, labourer.' He read the names out slowly. 'All known to us in various degrees. Kerjean and Bola were in the van. Duchesne was with Orega. Nosjean says there was another one, but he seems to be missing. There were five in the park. We've got four. One's disappeared.'

'Got his name?' Pel asked.

'No. And they're not talking.'

They never did, of course. It was more than life was worth for people like Jean-Pierre Orega to split on a confederate.

'Let's try again,' Pel said. 'You take first bite.'

They had the van driver, Kerjean, in first but he continued to insist that he hadn't been involved in any robbery. The van he'd been driving, he said, was just what it seemed to be – a van about its lawful business. They got nothing from him, not even the name of the fifth man who had been with them in the Parc de la Columbière.

'I didn't see no fifth man,' Kerjean said.

'He was there,' Darcy snapped. 'He was seen by two police officers. Sitting with you.'

'There was a type sitting in a chair near by, but he wasn't with us.'

'So *you* were there?'

'Yes.'

'And you were planning the operation, weren't you?'

'What operation?'

'Orega's grab at Merciers.'

'We weren't in that!' Kerjean was shrill with indignation. 'We just happened to be in the van further down the street.'

'What was all the fuss about then?'

'What fuss?'

'All that climbing in and out. Getting yourself seen.'

'The van wouldn't start.'

'Why the disguises then? You look as if you were going to hold up the bank.'

Kerjean put on a big show of looking startled. 'Bank? Me? They weren't disguises. They were scarves. I pulled mine up over my mouth because it was cold. I've got thin blood.'

They knew Kerjean was lying but it was impossible to break him. He was clearly not going to admit to being part of Jean-Pierre Orega's robbery. He even had a good chance of getting away with it when it came before the magistrates.

'Somebody was behind it,' Pel decided. 'Orega couldn't organize a refuse collection, and this was as elaborately staged as the *Folies Bergère.*'

Nevertheless Orega declined to incriminate anybody else. They could have offered a reward, even perhaps the Legion of Honour and dinner with Brigitte Bardot, but he wasn't talking. He claimed he had set up the operation just for himself and Duchesne.

'Kerjean and Bola were seen with you in the Parc de la Columbière. You were seen synchronizing watches.'

Orega shook his head. 'I remember looking at the time and thinking it was getting late.'

'There was another man. A fifth man. Who was he?'

'I never saw any fifth man. I didn't even see these other two you keep going on about.'

They worked over the four of them for a long time but if there were an eleventh commandment designed especially for villains it was 'Though shalt not split on thy friends'. 'They were *all* in it,' Darcy snarled. 'They're all well known. All except for the fifth man. Why was *he* there?'

Nosjean and De Troq' hadn't got the number of his car because he hadn't had one. He had left with Orega. And for most of the time he had had his back to them so that their description was vague. Tall, thin, large nose, fair hair, wearing a red and green windcheater. That was the best they could manage. And now he seemed to have disappeared.

An identikit picture was put together and a police artist's impression of the missing fifth man was soon available. Pel studied it carefully.

'He must have been recruited to get rid of the loot,' he said. 'But, as the loot doesn't seem to have reached him, he's innocent until we can talk to him and find out if we can charge him with conspiracy.'

Pel and Darcy were coming away from giving the Chief the latest on the case when Claudie Darel appeared, to inform them that a young woman was in Pel's office wishing to talk to him.

Immediately they discovered they had yet another case on their hands, this time even more serious than a hold-up. A murder, no less. The young woman was not much more than twenty, pretty, but with a knowing look about her. She sat in the chair Darcy held out by Pel's desk, while Pel thought bitterly that the evil-doers who dwelt on the earth's surface never gave much thought to the hard-worked police. They never managed to clear the board of one crime before another appeared. With just a little consideration, he felt, life could have been so much easier.

The girl had a worried look and they thought perhaps she was in shock. In fact, it was something else entirely.

'To think we were going to do *that*,' she said, 'right alongside *that*.'

Pel eyed her for a moment, his expression unchanged. He had seen and heard enough during his career not to be startled by anything.

'I knew there was something wrong,' she went on in a rush. She touched her bosom. 'I felt it — here. I knew there was somebody in the bushes. I felt it all the time.'

'Why?'

'I don't know. I just did.'

'Did you see anybody else there? Any men?'

'Just the one who was with me. He seemed to have six pairs of hands and I was fighting them all off. I landed him

31

one on the jaw. That stopped his gallop.'

Pel glanced at Darcy. They had guessed what the girl had been up to in the woods and now she had made it plain.

'And what happened?'

'I let out a yell. Something about "There's a foot in it!" I'd thought the shoe was just one somebody had lost. But when it wouldn't move, I knew why. I was scared, believe me.'

'Of course you were. So your boy-friend went off to tell the police?'

'No, he didn't. I did. He was all for getting in the car and going home and forgetting all about it. But in the end he said he would. Then I found he hadn't done anything at all, so I thought I'd better do it. I'm a bit late but here I am.'

'We're grateful,' Pel said. 'We'd better have your name.'

'Vera Vixen.'

'Mademoiselle?'

'Madame. Not that it matters. My husband walked out on me a year ago. I'm free to do as I please.'

'And the man you were with?'

'Do I have to tell you?'

'At this point it's not important. Why *didn't* he come and inform us?'

Vera Vixen gave what was remarkably like a snort of disgust. 'Because he's married,' she said. 'And, because, in spite of his big talk, he's as yellow as they come. He was scared stiff.' She smiled maliciously. 'Actually, his name's Robert Flandres, if you really want to know, and he lives in Louze and he works at Electronics Bourguignons, where I work. I don't see why he shouldn't be in it, too. Will his name be in the paper?'

An hour later Vera Vixen peered through the rear window of the police car at the small group of men standing near the patch of undergrowth. One of them was on his knees poking at the soil. Another car stood alongside the one in which she sat and, even as she watched, yet another drew up and Grenier, the police photographer, climbed out. Within five minutes several other cars, summoned by radio, had arrived, together with a van from which screens and orange-coloured tape and metal stanchions were produced. Hands were shaken and, as she watched, the group of men were blocked from her view by plastic sheets.

'Any indication who she is?' Pel was asking.

Leguyader, the head of the Forensic Laboratory at the Medico-Legal Institute, looked up. 'No,' he said. 'Nothing.'

'Let's have a description.'

Doctor Minet, the police surgeon, sniffed. 'One hundred and sixty centimetres. Female. White. Blond hair going grey but dyed. Fortyish, I'd say. Mature. One of the fingers has been nibbled by some wild animal − perhaps a weasel or a rat.'

To Vera Vixen the men among the trees seemed to be doing a lot of talking when she felt they should be rushing about arresting people. She was disappointed when she was driven back to the city, so she decided to take the rest of the day off and go into the office the following morning, claiming she'd been working with the police for hours. She'd have plenty to tell her colleagues. She would also, she decided, ask to be allowed to work with somebody other than Robert Flandres.

Pel watched the car go, then turned his attention back to the shallow hollow in the ground and its grisly contents. Now that the body had been disturbed, the smell of putrefaction was marked and the air was loud with the sound of flies. They bent again over the grave − Pel, Leguyader and his assistant, and Doctor Minet and Doctor Cham.

'When?' Pel asked.

The body was in a fragile state and they were pulling away the soil with gloved hands. 'Five to six weeks,' Cham said. He indicated turves they had removed. They'd been laid over the body in a hurry and some had been upside-down. The grass on them had turned yellow and was withering. 'Rough estimate, of course. Shallow burial. Done in a hurry, I'd say.'

'Clothing tell us anything?'

'I get the impression of quality,' Leguyader said. 'But, somehow, not a lot of money. I'll tell you more when we get them to the laboratory and examine them in more detail.'

'Not sexual,' Doc Minet added. 'Her underclothes haven't been disarranged. The back of the skull's stove in.

'What with?'

'Iron bar. Wooden pole. Stake. Car jack. Sledge-hammer.' It pleased Minet to be sarcastic. 'Something like that. Hard and heavy. I think —' he paused, 'I think she was dragged in here some time after she was killed. One of the shoes is missing. I suspect she was killed then left for a while, because whoever did it was in a panic and wanted to get away. But then he — or she, of course — came back and tried to hide her. There are marks on her cheek as if she's been dragged along the ground. The flies had been at her by then, of course. She's literally crawling with maggots now. We'll need to give her a bath in disinfectant to kill them before we can examine her.'

There wasn't much else they could do before the reports from Doc Minet and the laboratory arrived but, in the meantime, everybody who could be spared was searching the area carefully. The other shoe was not found, nor was a handbag or any of its contents.

'Probably taken deliberately to hide her identity,' Darcy suggested. 'Unlike men, women don't carry their identity about their person. You've only to remove a woman's handbag and she immediately becomes anonymous because that's where her identity lives.'

'It *could* be that the handbag was in her car,' Pel said. 'Or

34

his car, the car of whoever did it – and when he or she fled in a panic it went with them. If she had it with her, of course. After all, why would a woman want a handbag in the Forêt de Diviot? If it *was* there, then I don't suppose it exists any more. It'll have been burned or buried or something. Nothing on the shoe?'

'Prélat, of Fingerprints, shook his head. 'Nothing, *patron*. Shoes don't usually show much. They're Bally shoes and you can buy them anywhere. No fingerprints. There very often aren't. You've probably noticed women slip shoes on by putting their toes in, then pulling them into place with a finger tucked inside the heel. Whichever way it was done, there are no prints.'

So that was that and they had to possess their souls in patience because Missing Persons had had no one reported missing in the last two months who fitted the description they had.

'On the other hand,' Darcy pointed out, 'she was probably a runaway wife and didn't *want* to be found.'

'She wouldn't be walking, though, would she?' Pel said. 'Not in those shoes. So how did she get there? It's ten kilometres from Vieilles Etuves and twenty from St-Siméon. And it's not the sort of place where women go walking alone. She must have driven there – in which case, where's her car? Or been driven there – in which case, who was the driver? And where is he now? And why did he do her in? Which brings us back to the original question: who is she?'

3

Doctor Cham, who was Doc Minet's assistant, appeared in Pel's office. With him was Leguyader, of Forensic. They had been working together, which was always a sound and sensible idea but didn't happen very often with peace and harmony. Leguyader was as difficult to handle as Pel himself and always delighted in turning up something that would throw a spanner in the works. Working in close co-operation with someone as young, modern and stubborn as Cham seemed to calm him down a little.

Cham was holding a large brown envelope containing the report he and Doc Minet had compiled. He was a tall young man with glasses and a long neck with a protruding Adam's apple. He wasn't much to look at but they'd discovered he had a quick perceptive brain and they'd all decided he was just the man to take Doc Minet's place when the old man finally retired.

'There's no sign,' he reported, 'that she had recently had sex, and she certainly wasn't pregnant.'

Well, if nothing else, that meant she hadn't been murdered because she was carrying an unwanted child.

Leguyader was hopping about like a dog wanting to be let out and Pel recognized the sign. He had something to say he considered important. Perhaps he'd got it from the *Encyclopédie Larousse* which, it was believed, he perused every evening for something new with which to dazzle the

Philistines at the Hôtel de Police.

'We've done a preliminary examination of the clothing,' he said. 'It wasn't disturbed and it's all French —'

'Shouldn't it be?'

'No,' Leguyader snapped. 'Not necessarily. In fact — if you'll allow me to finish — there was, as I was about to say, one exception, a cotton and acrylic sweater. It's marked *St. Michael.*'

'They're calling sweaters after saints?' Pel knew very well what *St. Michael* meant but he could never resist putting Leguyader off his stroke with an interruption.

Leguyader sniffed. 'It's the maker's name,' he said coldly. 'And I happen to know it's English. The people who manufacture and sell them are Marks and Spencer, a British supermarket group.'

'So she could be English?'

'Again, not necessarily.' Leguyader was at his most pedantic. 'She could be Scottish. Or Welsh. Or Irish. Or French even. They have a store in the Champs Elysées in Paris. This I know because the last time I was there I was dragged in to re-equip the family with new clothes. They may also have a store in Marseilles and doubtless in other places, too. On the other hand —' Leguyader paused, 'the sweater *may* have been bought at a store in England.'

'Any other indication that she's English?'

'Not at the moment,' Cham said. 'Her teeth will probably tell us. They have different methods of tooth care in England and use different amalgams for fillings. I'll check.'

'Nothing else?'

'Nothing we can see. She wears a wedding ring, but we think that's French. She *could* be a tourist. It happens occasionally. Husbands or lovers getting rid of unwanted women. Take them on a visit to romantic Paris, suggest a trip into the country and leave them there.'

'Sometimes they're left there by Frenchmen,' Pel said drily. 'They strike up a romance and it proves awkward.' He scowled, because he knew it could be a whole lot simpler even than that. Tourists had been murdered by over-sexed farm boys they'd never met before. But this time it didn't seem to involve sex because the woman's clothing had not been removed or damaged or even disarranged.

There was the Chief to inform, and the Procureur who would have to assign an examining magistrate to work with the police. Then there was the Press. There was always the Press, coming down like wolves on the fold, usually demanding information that couldn't be given.

Their first questions, of course, were the usual ones.

'Is it a rape case, Chief?' Sarrazin asked. Sarrazin was a free-lance who represented half a dozen Paris and provincial papers, mostly of the gutter type, and could always be relied upon to have his eyes open for anything faintly salacious.

'At the moment,' Pel said, 'it doesn't appear to be.'

'Who is she?'

'Your guess is as good as mine.'

They went off, satisfied, and the following day's headlines came well up to expectation, GIRL'S BODY FOUND. 'Girl?' Pel said. 'Name of God, she was forty if she was a day.' LOVE NEST NEAR BY? 'It is believed,' Sarrazin's papers announced, 'that, though her name isn't known, the victim was living in the area of Vieilles Etuves and that she had been seen in a car with a man.'

Pel shrugged. Newspapermen in France were never known for their veracity. Sometimes they helped the police by frightening a suspect out of hiding or into doing something silly, but mostly, apart from giving the great sporting public a salacious half-hour, they did nothing to forward a case.

He frowned at his blotter. You could count the reasons for murder, when you boiled them all down, on the fingers of one hand. And the sooner the police got on the trail the better it was. If they could be informed within an hour they invariably found the killer close to the scene of the crime, shocked and speechless. If the trail was a few hours old, it was that much harder. Six weeks was almost impossible. The killer could be in the South of France by then. In the United States. In China. In outer space. It was surprising who got to outer space these days.

So, he thought, if it weren't a matter of sex, what was it? There was always unrequited love — which included jealousy and fury — and greed. When you thought about it, there weren't many more.

Somehow, though, despite the missing handbag, Pel had a feeling it wasn't robbery. So why had she been murdered? It had all the signs of a premeditated affair. The spot where she was found was about as isolated and unpopulated as you could get. Even in summer there were few people in the forest. A hunter or two, perhaps, anxious to shoot anything that moved — a rabbit, a starling; even, sometimes, another hunter. Even when their lives were not being threatened, Frenchmen with guns were quick on the draw.

He was still sitting at his desk, gloomily pondering the problem, when Aimedieu appeared. He was another of Pel's bright young men who, like Nosjean and De Troq', were expected to go a long way.

'I've just brought in Philippe Bigeaud, *patron*,' he said.

Pel sighed. Bigeaud was a deviate well known to the police. He was always being brought in for indecency or trying to molest young girls.

'Well, get rid of him,' he snapped. 'Shove him up before the magistrates. You don't need me to tell you what to do. He's always being brought in. What was it this time?'

Aimedieu refused to be put off. 'Loitering,' he said.

Pel's head lifted. 'You mean, looking for some kid to frighten?'

Aimedieu stuck to his guns. 'No, *patron*, not this time. He said he was hiding. He was in that abandoned house near the waste ground at the end of the Rue de la Poésie. He lives round there.'

'Hiding?' Pel said slowly.

'That's what he said, *patron*.'

'Who from?'

'He said he was a witness to that house fire there two months ago. He said he saw who did it and that the man who did it knew he was seen and by whom. So Bigeaud's been trying to keep out of his way ever since.'

Pel remembered his talk with Darcy. 'Does this type he saw, whoever he is, also live near the Rue de la Poésie?'

'Bigeaud doesn't know. But, since he saw him there, he thought he might.'

Pel pushed his chair back. The house in the Rue de la Poésie, Darcy had discovered, was owned by a Dutch couple. There were several other Dutch families in the area who owned houses and a lot of resentment among the locals because of it. It began to seem that Darcy's idea that the fire had been deliberately started was not so far out. But it didn't seem the Dutch couple were involved because they had been found to be under-insured and had lost all their furniture.

'Let's go and ask him a few questions,' he said.

Bigeaud was sitting in the interview room, twitching at his trousers. He was a lean, pale-faced man with a long neck and a bad case of acne. He jumped to his feet as Pel entered.

'I was only hiding,' he said at once.

Pel waved to him to sit down and took a chair opposite him.

'Hiding from what?' he said.

'This man.'

'Which man?'

'This type I saw set the house on fire.'

'How did you see him?'

'Well —' Bigeaud hesitated, 'I was just walking by —'

'Time?' Pel glanced at Aimedieu.

'Midnight, *patron*.'

'Just when everybody goes to bed. Any young women

40

round there?'

Aimedieu grinned. 'Plenty.'

'He was Peeping Tomming, I suppose.' Pel gestured at Bigeaud. 'What do *you* say you were doing there?'

'I couldn't sleep,' Bigeaud said earnestly. 'I often can't. So I go for a walk.'

Pel didn't believe him for a minute. Criminals and deviates didn't change. Their habits remained the same; they just grew more so as they grew older.

'So what did you see?' he asked. 'Apart from women going to bed.'

'I wasn't looking for —' Bigeaud stopped dead because he knew he wasn't believed. 'I was under the trees. It was dark. I saw this man come past. He was carrying a can and I smelled petrol. He stood and looked about him. I think he was deciding which way the wind was blowing. Then he vanished. I was scared he was the brother of one of the —'

'The girls you'd been watching?' Pel finished for him.

'No. I wasn't, sir. Not really. I —'

Pel gestured wearily. 'Go on about this man.'

'Soon afterwards I saw flames in the house. I thought he must have started it.'

'But you didn't inform the fire brigade?'

'No. I was scared.'

'Name of God, you idiot! You might have saved the place!' Pel sighed and lit a cigarette. 'All right, go on. What next?'

'As I stepped out from under the trees, I almost bumped into him. He was running. I smelled petrol again. Then I knew he'd done it. He saw me, though. He got a good look at me.'

'Didn't you tell *anyone*?'

'No. I bolted. Into the darkness. I found some bushes and lay flat underneath them. I heard him moving about and knew he was searching for me.'

'Who was he? Do you know?'

'Yes.'

'Well? Name?' Pel was growing impatient.

'I think it's André Corvo. He's a carpenter. I've seen it on the van he drives.'

Pel glanced at Aimedieu. 'Take him away,' he said. 'But hang on to him for a while. We might need him for corroboration. In the meantime, let's have this André Corvo in.'

Corvo was a hard-faced angry young man and his answer was brisk and unequivocal. Faced with the information that he was believed to have set a house on fire, he admitted it at once with an air of defiance.

'I was going to buy that house,' he said bitterly. 'I made an offer and it was accepted. But then these bastards from Holland came along and offered a higher price. And the lousy con who owned it took their money and went to live in Brittany. Now, when we marry, me and my girl will have to go and live with my mother. None of us fancy that and it's about thirty kilometres from where I work and from where we want to live.'

'Were your intentions to buy the damaged house cheaply and make something of it?'

'I can't afford that. But the Dutch lot can. They'd submitted plans to convert it to a modern dwelling. People like me haven't a chance. This is *our* country, not some Dutch speculator's. It's not surprising it goes on all the time.'

Pel's eyes narrowed. 'What goes on all the time? Arson?'

'It must do. A guy even offered to do it for me.'

Pel sat up sharply. '*Offered?* Does he make a profession of it or something?'

'He said he knew all about it.'

'Who was he? Have you his name?'

'You don't think he'd tell me, do you?'

'Did he ask for money?'

'No.'

'What did he look like, this man?'

'Tall. Thin. Big nose.'

'Dark or fair?'

'Fair.'

'Did he say he'd done it before?'

'Yes.'

'Houses?'

'Anything. He said it was easy. I think he'd had a few drinks and was showing off.'

'Where did this meeting take place?'

'In the street. He just stopped me. After the Dutch bought the house. I didn't take any notice of him. I thought he was just shooting his mouth off.'

'But perhaps he wasn't, was he? Why did he approach *you*? You haven't been advertising, I suppose. In the small ads column of *Le Bien Public*: "Wanted – expert fire raiser."'

Corvo scowled. 'I suppose he heard me shouting the odds in the bar. I have been doing.'

'Which bar?'

'The Bar Emilien in Talant. That's where I usually go. We're always talking about houses there. We're mostly in the building trade and we mostly work in and around Talant and some of us are wanting to buy. We get a bit fed up.'

Pel turned to Aimedieu. 'Check that bar. Get names and look them up. Somebody might know our friend's adviser on arson.' He swung in his chair back to Corvo. 'The fact that you're helping us now won't stop us putting you up before the magistrates,' he said. 'You realize that, don't you?'

Corvo's scowl grew deeper. 'I don't suppose I'll be getting married now.'

'Not this year, you won't. Arson isn't the answer. Will your girl wait?'

'I think so. She knew what I did. I told her.'

'What did she say?'

Corvo answered wearily. 'She told me I was mad.'

'She was right.'

'I was just so fed up. We'd been waiting ages. I was furious that somebody with more money from another country had got the house we'd set our hearts on.'

Pel lit a cigarette. Slowly, to give him time to think. 'You know St-Etois?' he asked.

Corvo looked sourly at him, resenting the questioning. 'I've worked there. On the housing estate that's going up.'

'Know the woods there?'

'We used to drive out there to eat our sandwiches in the lunch break. It caught fire.'

'We think somebody *set* it on fire. Was it you?'

Corvo's eyes opened so wide they looked as though they might fall out and roll about the floor. 'No,' he yelled. 'It wasn't! I've admitted this one and I expect I'll get it in the neck for it, but don't start hanging any others on me!'

'What about this other type? Did *he* mention St-Etois?'

'No, he didn't!'

'He might have been interested though, mightn't he? Why didn't you report him to us? We need to pull him in. He might have done the St-Etois job. He might even be offering to do a similar job for other people, too. What's more, his offer might be taken up. Let's have a description of him. Every detail. Everything you can remember.'

They got the identikit man in and started work. Within an hour they had a picture of the volunteer incendiary. To Pel he looked remarkably like the picture they'd built up of the missing man from the team that Jean-Pierre Orega had been briefing in the Parc de la Columbière.

'Get hold of Nosjean,' he said.

When Nosjean arrived, accompanied as usual by De Troq', Pel handed him the identikit picture.

'Seen that type before?' he asked.

'Sure, *patron*. That's the type we saw with Orega in the park. The fifth man. The one we thought might be a fence.'

'Found out any more about him?'

'Nothing, *patron*. He seems to have vanished. Where did this come from?'

'A type called Corvo.'

'Does he know him?'

'Not by name.'

'Is he involved in another job?'

'Yes and no. It seems that whatever else he does for a living, he also specializes in setting things on fire on the side.'

4

The atmosphere at the Chief's conference was tense. It seemed that as usual, like a juggler, they had half a dozen balls in the air and were trying to keep them all going at once.

'Think this Rue de la Poésie fire's got any connection with this deliberate burning of the woods?' the Chief asked.

'It might well have,' Pel said. 'We've been doing a little checking up. Aimedieu got the names of everybody who uses the Bar Emilien. He's going round them now. Some of them remember this type who made his offer to Corvo but they don't know his name. He's a stranger.'

'It was a damn funny offer to make.'

'Perhaps he was out of work.'

'Did he make the offer to anybody else in the bar?'

'Apparently not. But that's probably because land isn't involved. Several others are after homes, but they want flats or city dwellings. You could put three or four houses on the land attached to the one in the Rue de la Poésie that Corvo wanted. Perhaps that was the attraction. Perhaps he knew somebody who might be interested. After all, there seems to be quite an influx of foreigners these days. People are even starting to complain. Maires are refusing permission for the sale of houses to them. You've read of Honfleur.'

The Chief *had* read of Honfleur.

'They claimed there that when the foreigners arrived

there — not in ones and twos but in floods — they started modernizing the old buildings they'd bought so that there was a danger of the whole character of the place being altered. It's happened in other places. Here, for instance. At St-Lazare-en-Bleu we have a colony of Dutch. At Garnier there's a colony of British. At Etang de Colonne they're Germans. *They*'re just the large groups. But there are other smaller ones around — Swiss, Belgians, Americans. Thanks to Monsieur Gorbachev, we can doubtless at any moment expect groups from Russia, Czechoslovakia, Yugoslavia, Poland, Bulgaria, Azerbaijan and Outer Mongolia.'

The Chief sighed. 'It won't change either,' he admitted. 'If anything, it'll get worse. The Common Market's made living abroad easier.'

Pel gestured at Darcy who had been making enquiries of his own.

'I had a talk with Bernaud's, the estate agents,' he said. 'They filled in the picture a bit. Foreigners like to buy homes close to each other. Where one Englishman or one Dutchman buys, another turns up. The estate agents mention there's a compatriot there and it becomes a selling point. So it ends up with them gathering their friends around them and another little colony springs up.'

The Chief was a fair-minded man. 'Surely it isn't just the foreigners' fault. After all, it's French people who're selling.'

Darcy smiled. 'Bernaud's say the farmers are falling over themselves. They sell their property then retire to the nearest town and buy themselves a house in the suburbs with all mod. cons., leaving the buyers to deal with the lack of facilities they put up with for generations. It's big business. Houses are expensive in England; here they're being offered as bargains.'

'*Are* they bargains?'

'They look like bargains in the British newspapers. Bernaud's showed me a few. They don't mention that they have no electricity, no mains drainage and no piped water.

And, having landed themselves with a lot more expense than they bargained for, the buyers then find they're lonely. So they encourage their friends to buy, too, and — *houplà!* — *another* colony springs up. In the south they're actually producing brand-new complexes disguised as Spanish fishing villages. There's a speculator in London, I gather, who specializes in this sort of thing and he has an associate here in France. It might be a good idea to find who he is.'

The Chief frowned. 'Building isn't against the law,' he pointed out.

'Burning woodland is,' Pel said quietly.

'So,' Darcy added, 'is vandalizing empty farmhouses.'

Brochard's father was a small man with bright alert eyes that indicated there wasn't much he didn't know and hadn't seen.

'That Barthelot,' he said, 'is about as straight as a corkscrew. A bent corkscrew. You've heard of Sebastien Croquis?'

Full of his mother's food and his father's wine, Brochard sat back, lethargic but with his mind in top gear. 'Who's Croquis?'

'Keeps that farm at Valdegil. You know the one. Looks as though it's been hit by a hurricane. Bad farmer. Had a few of my sheep in his time.'

'Stole them? Did you inform the police?'

'Didn't bother. I got some red cotton from your mother and threaded it through the tails of twenty or thirty of my animals. You couldn't see it but it was there if you knew where to look. Then I told the tannery at Engentil to keep a look-out for fleeces that came from Croquis. When they told me some had turned up I got them to put them on one side. Some had the red cotton through their tails.'

'So?'

'Croquis is Barthelot's brother-in-law.'

'And is Barthelot the same?'

'I reckon so.'

The following morning, Brochard went to see Barthelot's neighbour, a man called La Verne, the man he had accused of killing his sheep.

'He wants to take over my land,' La Verne said.

'Would you sell?'

'Never. My family's been here since 1850.'

'He's accusing you of putting down poison for his sheep. Has he had autopsies done on them?'

'He says so. I don't believe him.'

'They seem to be dead, all the same. Is he insured?'

'Yes. Guillemard Assurance. One of their people came along asking questions.'

Barthelot turned out to be a big man with a fleshy face and eyes so small they seemed in danger of disappearing. Brochard introduced himself as a representative of the Guillemard Assurance Company.

'What's the trouble?' Barthelot demanded.

'Just checking,' Brochard said.

'There's no need. You've only to ask at the tannery at Engentil. They'll tell you how many of my ewes they've had. Breeding ewes too. Best Larzacs. I paid a fortune for them. That bastard over the hill poisoned them.'

'Why would he do that?'

'Because he dislikes me. He thinks I want to take him over. I do, as a matter of fact. He's a sloppy farmer.'

'His family's been at it for generations,' Brochard pointed out. 'I thought he wasn't bad.'

'What do you know about it?' Barthelot snorted.

Brochard smiled. 'I grew up on a farm,' he said.

The following day, by sheer luck, another of Barthelot's ewes died. Brochard's father brought the news and Brochard went along to the farm to claim the carcass.

'What do you want it for?' Barthelot demanded.

49

Brochard put on his innocent choirboy face. 'Just to check,' he said.

Taking the carcass back to his father's farm, Brochard and his father opened the animal up. His father laughed. 'Yew clippings,' he said. 'It's been eating yew clippings. I bet it's been eating them for ages. They're enough to knock over any sheep. Especially in this condition. It's a cross-bred and a pretty poor specimen at that. Barthelot doesn't know anything about farming. He always buys bad sheep.'

Brochard frowned. 'Where did the yew clippings come from?' he asked. 'I bet La Verne didn't feed them to it. The unmasticated bits look as if they've been cut deliberately with a knife.'

That afternoon, Brochard checked that La Verne hadn't a yew tree anywhere near his land. He then drove over to Barthelot's farm. Barthelot was at market so Brochard introduced himself to his wife and persuaded her to allow him to look around. 'Just a formality,' he said.

He noticed at once that there was a big yew behind the barn, close to the pens where Barthelot kept his lambs and close to where he kept his bales of hay. It had been cut back and there were a lot of fallen needles and clippings among the loose hay and on the ground, and several plastic bags of chemical fertilizer, one or two of them split.

'You feed hay to the sheep?' he asked.

'When the weather's bad,' Barthelot's wife said. 'We used to keep the lambs and the feed at the other side of the barn but my husband reorganized things. He trimmed the tree and moved the feed nearer, he says it saves him work.'

There was a horse in the paddock and Brochard leaned on the gate, admiring it.

'Nice animal,' he said.

'It's my daughter's.'

'Take a lot of looking after, horses. Hay, bran mash, chaff. All that. Have any problems with it?'

'It was off colour during the cold weather. When it was

50

on hay.'

'What do you cut chaff with?'

'There's a chaff cutter in the stable.'

'I haven't seen one of those for years.'

Affecting interest as a collector of old farming machinery, Brochard got permission to inspect the machine. Its four geared blades whirled at speed to the slow swing of the handle. Brochard admired it effusively. 'We had one of those when I was a boy,' he said. 'Why we didn't cut our fingers off I don't know.'

He moved round the machine, peering closely. Among the chaff on the floor he found yew seeds and needles, some of them chopped into small fragments.

He decided he had all the evidence he needed. All it required now were a few enquiries into Barthelot's background. But for the time being he had other things to do. Charlie Ciasca wasn't all that far away.

Driving to Lyons and joining the east-west motorway, he climbed out of his car by Charlie's flat, watched with interest by all the other girls with whom she shared accommodation. There seemed to be dozens of them.

'Come on in,' she said, grinning at him.

'With that lot?' he retorted indignantly. 'Why not somewhere alone?'

'I think you're after me.'

Brochard affected innocence.

'Most men are. And I know what they want.'

It was Brochard's turn to grin. 'Well,' he said, 'it's not a bad idea.'

'Haven't you got a girl?'

'I had. I broke with her.'

'Why?'

'She was too possessive. She said she'd shame me by taking an overdose of sleeping pills.'

'Did she?'

'No. But she said she'd set her brothers on to me. She has

51

two.'

'So have I.'

Brochard was startled.

'And like me, they're part-Swiss, part-Italian, part-French. Mostly Italian. And you know what the Italians are like. And, though the Swiss seem pretty placid people, they have hidden depths. They've been known to shoot at each other from time to time.'

'Even club each other with cuckoo clocks?'

'Even that. They have riots in Switzerland these days. Not many. But some. My brothers protect me. Gabriel and Jean-Jacques. They're tough.'

When Pel reached his office the following day, Darcy was waiting for him.

'We've had a dental report on the woman at Vieilles Etuves,' he said. 'The amalgam in the fillings isn't French. So, in view of the sweater she was wearing being British, the amalgam's probably British, too. We'll try the police there.'

As Darcy left there was a telephone call for Pel from Lyons. The line was bad and the accent was English. It turned out to be Superintendent Goschen, of Scotland Yard. He had helped Pel on previous occasions, and their respect was as mutual as the assistance they offered each other.

'Charles Goschen,' the ghostly voice said through a symphony of crackles and bangs. 'I'm in Lyons and I'll be passing through your patch.'

They had no difficulty talking because Pel spoke some English and Goschen some French and the extra bits they filled in with Franglais.

'I'm on my way north from Provence,' Goschen said. 'I've been on a little job down there and I thought it would be nice to call in and see you. You might even be able to help me.'

Remembering the magnificent hospitality he had

52

received from Goschen and his family on his rare visits to London on duty, Pel was immediately eager to respond in kind.

'You must stay with us,' he said. 'You mustn't think of anything else.'

When he telephoned his wife, in a panic at the shortness of notice, she received the news as calmly as she received all news of imminent disasters. He arrived home to find she had left her office early and was pottering in the kitchen. She was even singing, one of the strange little songs she seemed to enjoy so much.

'Chez nous, il y a trois petits chats,
Chaton, Chaton, Chatonette,
Chez nous, il y a trois petits chats —'

'He'll be here soon,' Pel urged.

'We're all ready,' Madame pointed out calmly.

Half an hour before Goschen was due to arrive, Pel was in the garden wearing the suit he kept for levees, meeting film stars and the President of France, or in case they ever gave him the Légion d'Honneur.

'Who're you looking for?' The speaker was Yves Pasquier, the small boy from next door. As usual, judging by the scratches and bruises on his legs, he'd been having a fight with a motor mower. He was accompanied by his dog. It resembled a dirty mophead and was so shaggy it was hard to tell which was the end that bit.

The boy obviously wanted to chat but, worried that his hospitality wouldn't measure up to what he'd received in London, Pel wasn't in the mood to bandy politenesses just then. Mornings, through a hole in the hedge, were the time when he usually held his conversations with Yves Pasquier.

'Aren't you doing your homework?' he asked.

'Done it.'

'Shouldn't you be taking the dog for a walk?'

'He's been. Who's coming?'

'How do you know somebody's coming?'

'They are, aren't they? I saw Madame Routy going off. She came back with a package that had obviously come from the butcher. I know the way he ties them up.'

'You'd make a good detective.'

'It wasn't just that.'

'Oh? What else?'

'You. You're in a state.'

Pel sniffed. 'It's a policeman,' he said.

'Do you usually put your best suit on for a cop?'

'He's an English cop.'

'Famous?'

'Oh, yes,' Pel said proudly.

'Would he give me his autograph?'

'I suppose so if you asked.'

'I'll get my autograph book.'

The boy was back within seconds and he and Pel stood in the garden watching the road with all the intensity of stout Cortez about to discover the Pacific.

It was not to be. Just as Pel spotted a car with a British number plate approaching, Madame Pasquier appeared and yanked her son indoors.

'You shouldn't let him bother you,' she said to Pel as she hauled him away.

'I want to stay,' her son screamed. 'It's a cop who's coming! He's famous! I want his autograph!'

'If you say any more I'll lock you in a cupboard full of spiders.'

The threat was greeted with derision. 'I like spiders. Their legs fall off when they're scared.'

Goschen reacted as Pel expected him to react — with British calm and British good manners. He admired Madame Pel — which wasn't very difficult; was pleasant to Madame Routy; gave his signature to Yves Pasquier who, having sneaked out while his mother wasn't looking, appeared at his side; even admired Pel's garden. On that point, of course, Pel knew he was just being polite. Pel had almost swooned over Goschen's garden in the London suburb where he lived. Goschen's lawn was like velvet and there were flowers, because Goschen was a gardener. Pel invariably found he had files to read or a stiff leg or a bad back when Madame mentioned *his* garden in the spring and autumn.

Madame surpassed herself with the meal and they didn't talk business until the following morning, when Pel insisted on Goschen's seeing the Chief, who was flattered enough to bring out the brandy bottle. Then he took him to lunch at the Relais Saint-Armand and they got down to talking shop over the liqueurs. 'I'm investigating a chap who's involved in a bit of shifty speculation,' Goschen explained and Pel's ears pricked up at once. 'He's been buying up land in England,' Goschen went on. 'Now we learn he's doing the same in France. He's a builder and he's working along the south coast near St. Tropez.'

Pel wondered if he were someone he might be interested in. 'Name?' he asked.

'Cornelius. Dirk Cornelius. We're not sure what nationality. He has a British passport but we think he might be Dutch.'

'Does he put up the money?'

'We think he's just the front man and there's somebody behind him. Some Spanish woman. Name of Carmen Vlaxi.'

Pel sat up sharply. 'It's not a she,' he said. 'It's a he.'

'You know him?'

'Half-Spanish, half-Arab. Came up from Spain. Worked things round Toulouse for a bit. Then he got ambitious and came north. Pretends to be Castilian. Known as Carmen the Bullfighter.'

'Is he now?'

'He tried to get into the Paris rackets but they were already pretty full and he hadn't enough clout to make himself stick, so he came here. We used to have a type called

Maurice Tagliatti, but you'll remember he was bumped off. You were involved. This Vlaxi took over his rackets, his territory and what was left of his troops. After we'd finished with them, there weren't more than one or two.'

Goschen grinned. 'That's what I like to hear. Does *he* go in for this building business?'

'What sort of building are you thinking of?'

'Well, this Cornelius acquires land. Usually cheaply because he puts the frighteners on the owners. Then he develops it. Leisure centres. Beach villages. You know – two hundred rabbit hutches painted white with a few trees and a swimming pool chucked in. Is that his scene?'

Pel was thoughtful. 'It might well be,' he said.

5

Pel was late leaving for the Hôtel de Police the following day. He had lingered over his breakfast coffee reading a report Goschen had left with him, so that he shot out of the house in a hurry and drove like a maniac for the city. As usual, as he hit the main road at the bottom of the hill from Leu where he lived, he was almost rubbed out by a lorry — and what a lorry! Eight wheels plus a trailer with another eight. As it appeared alongside him with a thunder that rattled his car, it was so tall he couldn't see the top of it, just the driver's mouth working as he called him names. There was nothing unusual about the incident — it happened regularly — but it shook Pel and he drove the rest of the way into the city as if treading on eggshells. The traffic cop on duty at the Porte Guillaume nodded gratefully as he passed. He knew Pel's driving and the fact that he was often deep in thought. More than once he had had to nip smartly out of the way.

Still faintly dazed, Pel headed for his office, too absorbed to return the '*Bonjour, patron*' of the man on the desk in the entrance. The man on the desk didn't take offence. It happened often.

'Silly con,' he said to himself.

Reaching his office, Pel sat down and stared at Goschen's report again.

Carmen Vlaxi. He turned the name over in his mind. They

hadn't heard much of him since his arrival in the area beyond the fact that he had a house at St-Symphorien-le-Grand and that he had a finger in more than a few pies. But nothing much had ever emerged. They hadn't pinned anything at all on him so far, though he'd be well worth watching if he'd got into this speculative building-for-foreigners business. That, to Pel, looked as though there might be a great deal of money in it. But no leisure centre, no holiday village complete with swimming pool and palms was worth going into for profit for people like Carmen Vlaxi unless the land was acquired dirt cheap. But — and this was the point — Carmen Vlaxi was just the type to know exactly how to acquire land at such prices. They'd heard he'd run a protection racket in the south near the Spanish border so it could be assumed he would know the ins and outs of putting pressure on people. After all, whatever the aim, the methods were much the same.

He was still debating it with himself when Darcy appeared.

'We've got a name,' he said.

Pel was still deeply involved in his mind with Carmen Vlaxi and the speculative builders and at first didn't grasp what Darcy was getting at.

'What for?'

'Not "what", *patron*,' Darcy pointed out. '"Who." The woman found at Vieilles Etuves. I think your good friend, Superintendent Goschen's been pulling a few strings for us.'

'I did happen to mention it,' Pel said modestly.

'Raby-Labassat,' Darcy went on. 'Bronwen Raby-Labassat. Aged forty.'

'Bronwen? That doesn't sound French.'

'It isn't. She was born in Cardiff in Wales. She married Honoré Eustache Raby-Labassat fourteen years ago. No children. Raby-Labassat has three, two sons and a daughter by a previous marriage. He's a baron.'

'Is he, by God?' Pel's interest grew. He would have loved

to be a baron himself. He always considered it a shame France had abolished titles.

'Lives at Faux-Villecerf,' Darcy continued. 'It's the other side of Aignay-le-Duc. Not much more than a hamlet. He has a chateau there.'

'Who put us on to her?'

'Local cop. Apparently her stepson, Auguste Raby-Labassat, reported her missing. She left home six weeks ago without saying why. Apparently it wasn't unusual. She liked to go back to London from time to time — occasionally without telling anyone. They thought that's where she was but when time dragged on, Auguste Raby-Labassat made enquiries of her family in Cardiff. They haven't seen her for over a year. So if she's been to London she didn't visit them.'

'Go on.'

'He decided he'd better contact the police, and the local cop — name of Morelot — remembered reading a report of the woman found dead at Vieilles Etuves. The description fits. The stepson thinks it might be his stepmother.'

Faux-Villecerf lay on the side of a hill overlooking a valley where the remains of the sunflower crop filled the fields. The area was well wooded and, below the road, the land fell away to flat water meadows full of buttercup and marsh marigold. Edged with celandine, the fields ran alongside the River Trine, which was one of a group of streams formed when the River Rinat, a tributary of the Saône, had been split into a sort of delta by the lie of the land. Further south, the streams joined up again near Dampierre-en-Sarve. Beyond the streams the land rose again to a wooded peak known as the Croq de Chien.

The village was small with narrow streets and looked quite dead in the afternoon sun. It wasn't dead, though, and Pel knew it wasn't. Eyes were watching through shutters closed against the heat as the car paused and they tried to find the entrance to the chateau.

It sat on its hillside above terraced gardens, the south side of the land ending in a flat-faced cottage with a large cowbyre and barn resting on a patch of grass buttressed by a high wall above the road. They could see the chateau above them, near the church, a solid block of masonry in the mellow ochre stone of the region.

The courtyard was dusty and hot and surrounded by stables and outhouses. As they stopped the car a door opened. It wasn't the main door, which was at the top of a flight of wide and imposing stone steps and looked heavy enough to require a squadron of dragoons to shift it. Instead, it was a small ill-fitting door half-obscured at the side of the steps. A policeman came out.

'Sous-Brigadier Morelot, sir,' he said.   As he spoke, another man stepped into the sunshine. He was square and solid and, although still young, was just beginning to go bald. He looked worried.

'I'm Auguste Raby-Labassat,' he said. 'You'll be the police. Come in.'

It was a blazingly hot day but immediately they were conscious of the coolness inside the house. They were led along a long dark hall to what appeared to be the kitchen. It was an enormous room full of ancient cupboards made of pine. There was a fireplace vast enough to house a couple of horses complete with stalls, mangers and probably a carriage as well. In front of it was a vast scrubbed table big enough to play football on and two easy chairs. 'Easy' wasn't really the word to describe them. They looked cheap, and as though they'd been picked up at a second-hand sale, and they matched neither in shape, woodwork or the colour of the fabric.

'The family mostly live in here,' Raby-Labassat pointed out. 'Because of the cost of heating. It's also handy for the garden and the courtyard.'

'Do *you* live here, Monsieur?' Pel asked.

'No. I live in Dijon. I'm an accountant. But I stay here regularly every summer.'

'For a holiday?'

'No. To cut the hedge.'

'To cut the hedge?'

Raby-Labassat gestured and, crossing to the window, they saw that the ground dropped rapidly away from them to give a magnificent view over the valley to the hills beyond. They could see fields quartering the slopes, clumps of trees and a long line of cypresses, like guardsmen in single file, marching up the hill. What Auguste Raby-Labassat was indicating, however, was an enormous box hedge that ran the whole length of the front of the chateau just beyond the terrace. It was nearly three metres wide, rising regularly in square blocks and arches like the castellations of a fortress to the height of four or five metres.

'I cut it twice a year,' Raby-Labassat said. 'Late spring and autumn.'

'What with?'

'Shears, a lot of it. We have an electric clipper but it's old-fashioned and heavy.'

'It must be hard work,' Darcy observed.

A shadow crossed the young man's face. 'I hate it,' he admitted. 'Even humping the ladders about is hard work. But it has to be done.'

'Couldn't you get one of these gardening firms in?' Darcy asked.

Raby-Labassat gave him a look that was a mixture of reproach and bitterness and it occurred to Pel that perhaps the family couldn't afford a gardener. A household that lived in the kitchen and worried about fuel bills might well be in straitened circumstances.

'My father will be here soon,' the young man said. 'I've asked him to be here.'

'Where is he?'

'He has a workshop in a cottage in the grounds. He

enjoys working in it.' Raby-Labassat paused. 'That woman,' he went on. 'The one at Vieilles-Etuves. It's Bronwen — my stepmother — isn't it?'

'We can tell better when we know more about her.'

'She was murdered, wasn't she? It was in the papers.'

'Yes, Monsieur. She was murdered.'

Raby-Labassat nodded, as if satisfied.

'While we're waiting,' Pel said, 'could you produce a photograph of your stepmother? It will not only help identify the woman we found but we can have it reproduced and use it to discover her movements.'

Raby-Labassat turned without a word and from a drawer produced a large photograph of his family. The Baron was a tall man with spectacles and a grim expression, as if he were standing before a firing squad. The Baroness, the missing Bronwen, was a good-looking, dark-haired woman, past her best but still attractive. There were three children with them, a spectacled teenaged girl and two older teenaged boys, one of whom was recognizable as Auguste Raby-Labassat.

'I dug it out,' Raby-Labassat said. 'When I heard you were coming.'

'That was thoughtful of you, Monsieur,' Pel said. 'Has your father any interests at Vieilles Etuves?'

'None at all. Of course, *she* might have had.' Raby-Labassat drew a deep breath. 'She married my father when he was no longer young. The marriage couldn't be called a success. They went their own ways.'

'What about your father? Did he — er — have other interests?'

'Yes.'

'What exactly?'

'Carpentry.'

Pel had been expecting anything but woodwork. But he blinked and recovered quickly. 'Would it be possible,' he asked,' to see your stepmother's room? It might help us a great deal.'

62

There was a moment of hesitation, then Raby-Labassat gestured at the door. 'This way.'

He showed them into a small room across the huge hall. It was furnished as a kitchen — a modern kitchen with a dishwasher, a washing machine, a stainless steel sink and an electric cooker.

'This is the kitchen she used,' he said. 'She used the old kitchen you saw as a living-room.' He opened a door and beyond they saw another small room containing a bed and a few toilet accessories.

'Is this your stepmother's room?'

Raby-Labassat flushed. 'It used to be the maid's. But we don't have a maid now. My parents used it. It's warm in winter.'

Pel's guess about the family had been a good one.

'Did she sleep here just in winter?'

'At first. She found the house cold. It can be very chilly in bad weather. It's so big and there's no central heating, of course. It would cost a fortune to install. So, soon after she married my father, she moved down here.'

There was no sign of anything male in the room. 'And your father?'

'He doesn't sleep here.' Raby-Labassat hesitated. 'They didn't agree and he had a room elsewhere.'

'I see.'

'My stepmother,' Raby-Labassat said in a stiff, disapproving way, 'ran things. My father wasn't interested. He preferred his carpentry. He was always buying bits of wood to repair doors and windows. He left things to Bronwen. And as she'd never previously run anything bigger than a rabbit hutch, she had no idea how to do it. She wasted money and damaged things. And it's my land.' He sounded bitter. 'My father said it was to be mine. He promised it. It wasn't hers to waste. She was always anxious to sell off a bit here or a bit there. To raise money.'

Raby-Labassat stopped dead as if he felt he'd said too

much. 'Would you like to see upstairs?'

He led the way along the stone-flagged hall. It was unlit by daylight except for a stone-mullioned window at one end and the glass in a door at the other, which seemed to lead into the garden. The hall smelled faintly of damp and was as cold as the tomb.

At the end, turning right, they faced a flight of stairs, three metres across, with wide treads and constructed of stone. It seemed to go away up into the heavens. At the top they could see an enormous chandelier.

'Originally, of course,' Raby-Labassat said,' the family all lived on the next floor and only the staff lived on the ground floor. But, of course, these days it's different.' He seemed to be faintly embarrassed.

At the top of the stone steps was another long hall with doors leading off. At the end, through glass doors similar to those below, was a huge balcony with a magnificent view over the valley. 'One of Theodore Archéatte's splendid creations,' Raby-Labassat said. 'It sticks farther out from the house than any other balcony in the province. Don't lean on the balustrade, though. It's old and I don't trust it.'

Pel peered over. Almost directly below him he could see the width of the vast box hedge that Auguste Raby-Labassat cut twice every year. No wonder he hated it. It must have presented a formidable task.

The young man was opening a heavy oak door. It led into a magnificent dining-room. It was papered in crimson and the walls were lined with enormous portraits of men and women in the dress of the 1870s.

'We don't use this place, of course,' he explained. 'It's kept just as my great-grandparents had it. My great-great-grandfather was governor of Tunisia for a time. That's him.'

He gestured at a portrait of a man whose fierce visage was festooned with moustaches and whiskers so that he looked like a tiger staring out of the undergrowth. He wore a high ear-slicing starched collar and cravat and across his breast a wide pink sash that was obviously part of some decoration. His wife, equally off-putting in expression, glared across the room at him from the opposite wall. The décor was mostly heavy Second Empire in style, with stuffed birds under glass domes and sepia photographs of the family and groups of soldiers obviously taken in North Africa.

Another door led into a salon. It was furnished in the same crowded fashion, with heavy bow-backed chairs and settees and more portraits of the same two people, but also now with a few younger people, even domestic pets. This room was a mixture of periods and it was clear the fittings and furnishings were all valuable but were all deteriorating slowly in the damp cold winters and hot summers of the region. The red glass chandelier obviously came from Murano.

'My great-grandfather was the man who went to Algeria to draw up a constitution in 1830,' Raby-Labassat said. 'His father was a general under the great Napoleon. Another ancestor was Maire of Dijon.' He jerked a hand at a painting of a man in a red robe. 'That's him.'

The coat of arms was quartered into devices of lions and stags rampant, arrows, flashes of lightning and palms, and bore the motto, *Unconquerable*.

Raby-Labassat gestured at his feet. 'The floors were all made here in Faux-Villecerf,' he said. 'From wood that came from the Forêt de Diviot. So was that.' He gestured at an enormous wardrobe that was ceiling-high and looked big enough to hold a circus in.

'It's Louis Quinze,' he said. 'The one next door's Louis Seize. The furniture in the kitchen – the big old objects – is Henri Second.'

They were shown into the study of the great man. The carpet was clearly valuable, as was a tapestry hanging on one of the walls.

'He was the first baron,' Raby-Labassat said. 'Created by

Napoleon III for his work in Tunisia. My father's the fifth baron.'

The bedrooms were all filled with the same dismal display of period furniture, though there was one room that was furnished in the style of the Thirties and looked out on to the courtyard and the top of a huge and ancient fig tree.

'My grandmother's room,' Raby-Labassat explained. 'She's dead now. After my grandfather died, she went to live in Dijon but when she visited us she always lived in this part of the house. She remembered the place as it used to be, of course, and refused to allow any change. She always insisted on a fire in her room in winter. My father created this room for her. It has the sun all day. He's very good with his hands.'

'Do-it-yourself?' Darcy asked.

The young man smiled. 'He's known in the village as "Monsieur Bricolage". You can get into the courtyard by the stone staircase. The door at the end of the hall opens on to it and there's a separate staircase my grandmother used. She was a heavy smoker and used to do it in bed. She once set the curtains on fire and had to be rescued. She wasn't in a lot of danger but the room was full of smoke. After that she demanded a fire escape, so my father built one.'

He unlocked the glass doors to a small balcony. From it a small wooden staircase led down to the garden. Pel glanced at Darcy. Both of them were wondering what would have happened if the flames had spread to the staircase.

As they talked, they heard a car arrive in the courtyard. It was very noisy and Pel wondered if that was Louis Quinze or Louis Seize, too.

'That will be my father.' Raby-Labassat turned. 'I'd better go and meet him. You'll have to forgive him if he seems vague. He's getting old and he's had a lot of worries lately. He also –' He gestured with his hand as if he were lifting a glass to his mouth. 'Just a little. He's all right but I have to watch him. Perhaps you'll follow me down.'

As he vanished, Darcy looked at Pel. They were both

aware of the chill in the rooms and were wondering what it must be like in winter when the winds from the east and north blew through the place.

Pel sniffed and rubbed his nose, convinced by the chill about him that the cold he had been expecting had definitely arrived. 'I didn't seem to notice the Baron's room,' he said quietly. 'Did you?'

6

Baron Honoré Eustache Célestin Raby-Labassat de Bur — it took a few minutes to get it straight and Pel was pleased to see someone else suffered from the administrations of an ambitious mother — was a tall stooping man with wispy grey hair and vague eyes. He was by no means everybody's idea of a baron. Most people expected barons to be erect, slightly military and commanding. This one was dressed in a shabby jersey with a worn hole where his stomach was situated, and a pair of rumpled cord trousers that looked as though they'd been slept in. He wore thick spectacles and was hesitant and distant, as though he didn't really belong in the world.

'Forgive me,' he said. 'I was occupied and I forgot the time. I understand you might have found my wife.'

'It seems so, Monsieur,' Darcy said. 'We still have to confirm it. You can probably help us.'

'In what way? I understand she's been lying in the earth a matter of two months.'

'Almost,' Darcy agreed. He described the sweater the body had been wearing and the Baron sighed and glanced at his son. 'It will be hers,' he said slowly. 'She possessed several. She bought them in England. You may check her drawers and wardrobe if you wish.'

'It will be necessary, I think. Can you explain how she came to be at Vieilles Etuves?'

'*I* can,' Auguste Raby-Labassat said.

The Baron regarded his son with sad reproachful eyes. 'Auguste,' he said in mild protest.

His son swung round on him. 'Father, these gentlemen are policemen. She was murdered. Whatever she got up to, they must know. We have to find who killed her.'

'What *did* she get up to?' Pel put in quietly.

Auguste Raby-Labassat turned to him. 'She had boyfriends,' he said.

'Forgive me for asking, but is that the reason why she slept downstairs and your father slept elsewhere?'

'Yes.'

'We didn't notice any of the bedrooms upstairs in use.'

'They aren't,' Raby-Labassat snapped. 'He doesn't sleep here.'

'Where does he sleep?'

The Baron came to life again. In between coming to life he seemed to be uninterested and even half-asleep. 'I have a cottage in the grounds.'

'And you live there?'

'Yes.'

'All the time?'

'Yes.'

'You do your own cooking?'

'No. I have a housekeeper.'

'Marie-Hélène Gaussac,' Auguste said shortly. 'She was housekeeper here until we could no longer afford to pay her.'

'Do you pay her now then?'

'No.'

The Baron seemed to vanish. One moment he was there, the next he had gone. Darcy was about to fetch him back when Auguste gestured. 'Leave him,' he said. 'I'll tell you. I think it upsets him.'

'What does?'

'What happened.'

'What did happen?'

'He was born here. So were his father and grandfather. Marie-Hélène Gaussac came as a maid when he was in his teens. I believe she was quite pretty. They fell in love. But, of course, there was no question of their marrying. My father was the future baron. Marie-Hélène was the daughter of a carter called Peignot. She became his mistress. When he married – he had to marry, of course, because of the title – she also married. A man called Gaussac. He used to beat her. He was killed in 1943 with the Resistance. After the war she returned here to help because my mother wasn't strong. She was very capable and took over the house. The servants had left because there was no money to pay them. When my mother died she and my father got together again. I personally fully approved. She's a splendid woman.'

Pel nodded. 'What about your brother and sister?'

'As they never come here what they feel doesn't seem to matter.' Auguste sighed. 'Then my father met Bronwen. She was a lot younger than he was and she swept him up on a visit he paid to England. It was a whirlwind romance and she married him. I think she tricked him into it. You've seen him. It wouldn't be hard. Poor Marie-Hélène was heartbroken. But she was loyal and stayed on. By that time, of course, we had become aware of the problems of keeping this place up. Bronwen had thought, because my father had a title, that he was wealthy, but all he has is this house and land and nothing very much to pay for its upkeep. They began to quarrel. My father – old Monsieur Bricolage – did a do-it-yourself job on one of the cottages in the grounds and eventually moved in there. Marie-Hélène moved in with him soon afterwards.'

'And this place?'

'Bronwen lived here. Marie-Hélène came in to clean from time to time.'

'Still?'

'Yes.'

'And this suited everybody?'

'My father was happy. So, I think, was Marie-Hélène. Bronwen, no. But there was a man in Beaune, I believe. There was one in Auxonne and one in Lyons. There may have been others.'

'Do you have names?'

'No.'

Which, Pel thought, was a pity because it was obviously a lead they would have to follow up.

Auguste Raby-Labassat was still speaking, his voice quiet and angry. 'She liked men. As much as anything because, since my father had no money, she couldn't afford to indulge herself and these other men were willing to. She was quite good-looking. I believe she was involved in some business deal with one of them.'

'What sort of business deal?'

'I don't know. Perhaps over this place. My brother and sister always felt it should be sold.'

'Did you?'

'No. Never.'

'Did you always disagree on this?'

'Always.'

'Strongly?'

'Yes.' Auguste sniffed in his priggish way at the mention of his brother and sister. 'Alain's not got the sweetest temper. He once wrecked a car when he found himself hemmed in, in a parking lot. He slammed his car back and forth until he could get out, then deliberately drove at the car that had hemmed him in. It cost him a lot of money. Someone saw him and took the number of his car.'

According to the inheritance laws, property in France had to be shared equally between all the children of a marriage. It was France's way of breaking up the big estates and went a long way towards explaining why France had so many large crumbling chateaux no one wanted. Pel wanted to know more about Auguste's wish to retain what seemed to

71

him a white elephant.

'You felt the family should hang on to the chateau?' he asked.

'*I* did. My brother and sister felt it should go.'

Pel glanced about him at the bare walls and stone floors. 'I imagine it wouldn't be easy to sell,' he murmured.

'I was against it all the time.'

'Supposing it *were* possible, would you still be against it?'

'Yes.' The answer was stiff. 'Because *I'll* be the next baron. When my father dies, the title comes to me. I know my brother sometimes uses the title, but he's not truly entitled to it. I will be. And my wife is pregnant. I expect to have a son.'

'You might have a daughter,' Darcy said in a flat voice.

'I doubt it. The Raby-Labassats have passed on their heritage from father to son for generations. This is the Raby-Labassat home. It's the family history. It's all here. I'll take care of it.'

Pel was inclined to wish him luck.

While they were still prowling round the place, Auguste's brother and sister arrived. They came separately and didn't appear to like each other very much. Alain Raby-Labassat was a thin young man with long hair who ran a small electronics firm during the day and a rock group in the evening. He wore his jacket like a cloak and a denim cap that was peaked and flat-topped and made him look like Lenin arriving in Russia to organize the revolution. His only interest in his father seemed to rest on how much he was worth. He had always, it seemed, agreed with his stepmother about the house.

'It's worth nothing,' he kept saying. 'We should unload it. There's still a little money left but this place's draining it away all the time. The Old Man's account's like a tank with a leak in it. What's in gets less every day. It's our job to plug the hole. And that means selling this place.'

'Does your father spend much on the upkeep?'

Alain Raby-Labassat laughed. 'Of course not. He does it himself. Isn't he Monsieur Do-it-yourself? Unfortunately, his eyes aren't what they were and his hands aren't steady any more and what he does never lasts. The plaster falls out. The putty doesn't stick. The paint's streaky. The wood warps. One of these days he'll kill himself falling off a ladder.'

'Did you see much of your stepmother?'

'Not all that much. Just occasionally. She tried to get me to help persuade the Old Man to get rid of the house. We all knew he hadn't a cat in hell's chance of getting much for it because nobody would want it. But at least it might have saved what's left of the family fortune.'

His sister, Philomène the Baron's daughter, held much the same views and they were intensified by the fact that, as she admitted, she was desperately in debt. She was a flat-chested young woman in a sort of string blouse that made her bust look like two oyster shells caught up in a net. She wore circular spectacles about the size of bicycle wheels. Her brother's small fawn-coloured Peugeot had been nothing to write home about; hers was a battered Deux Chevaux painted a psychodelic pink with flowers. She was suspicious immediately of Pel.

'You say you're a policeman?' she said.

'I'm quite confident I am,' Pel replied sharply.

She insisted on seeing their warrant cards which she examined with great care, turning them backwards and forwards, as if she thought they were forged. Eventually she consented to answer their questions.

'Getting rid of this place would make it possible for my father to help with my bills,' she said. 'I'm not married. I'm living in sin.' She made the announcement as if she expected the sort of reaction that would have greeted the Second Coming. 'My father disapproved of me because of that.'

Pel had a suspicion that there was more to it than that.

'All the same,' she went on, 'he sometimes gave me money. It was only when that damned Bronwen came that he grew tight-fisted. She influenced him against me. After all, my bills don't amount to much.'

'Too much,' Alain snapped. 'When this place's sold, it won't be just to pay your bills, believe me.'

'It isn't going to be sold,' Auguste said.

'Wouldn't an estate agent's fees for selling the place eat up what was left, anyway?' Pel asked mildly before they came to blows.

'Not,' Alain said sharply,' if my father just walked away from the place. There's no law that says you can't. It's far enough back from the road for things to fall off it without hurting anyone. It would just crumble. All he has to do is put a rope on stakes round the place with a notice — 'Danger. Keep Out.' He'd be within the law.'

'What do you reckon the place's worth?' Pel asked, a trace wistfully. He was a snob enough always to be impressed by grandeur, wealth and possessions. It had been his ambition as a young man to be so rich he would be able to bring his children to heel with the challenge, 'What's the matter? Don't you want my money?'

Darcy had no hesitation in giving his answer. 'To me,' he said, 'nothing. I wouldn't have it thrown at me. You wouldn't be able to move from the kitchen during the winter. The place's huge and it's falling down. The doors don't fit. The windows are warped. There are patches of damp everywhere.'

'Do you reckon the Baron could have killed his wife? For the life she was leading him?'

'I reckon,' Darcy decided, 'that he couldn't kill anything. Not even a rabbit.'

'What do you think of the children?'

'Not much. *They*'re a much better bet as suspects. Two of

74

them are grasping and think only of getting their hands on the old man's money. The other's so bloody formal I expect he shakes hands with his mistress before getting into bed with her.'

'They're not what you'd call a close and happy family, are they? That young man, Auguste, seemed to be throwing out hints that his brother could be violent enough to have killed his stepmother.'

'Not much point. He seems to have agreed with her. Perhaps Auguste did it himself and wants us to think it was Alain. At least, Bronwen was a threat to Auguste's future with her wish to sell off the place.'

'I'm interested in this Marie-Hélène Gaussac,' Pel said thoughtfully. 'I wonder what *she's* expecting to get out of it. So far she seems to have been the only one who's shown the Baron much loyalty. And there must have been something about *her* to have impressed him.'

They found Marie-Hélène Gaussac at the cottage the Baron had done up, a hundred metres from the house. It was a tiny place but it looked as though it would be a great deal warmer in winter than the house. She was old, like the Baron, but without doubt had once been pretty. In her face was a calmness they saw in none of the Baron's children. Somewhere around the place they could hear a hammer.

'It's Honoré,' she said. 'The Baron. He needs looking after all the time. It was obvious years ago he needed looking after. I've tried to do it.'

'Did you love him, Madame?'

'I've always loved him. From the first day I saw him. He was so helpless. It was instantaneous and it's never changed.'

'But you married —' Pel glanced at his notes, '— Marc-Marie Gaussac?'

'Why not? The man I wanted to marry was pushed into marriage by his father with someone he didn't love. She was a good woman. But she couldn't look after him. She was a

75

thin-blooded aristocrat — a De Gouchy. They're not much, but she wasn't a carter's daughter, so it was all right.'

'Would *you* have killed the new Baroness, Madame?'

The old woman looked frankly at them and gave them a bright-eyed smile. 'I could have,' she admitted. 'Often. But I didn't. I just ignored her.'

'And the future?'

'I'll go on looking after him just as long as I can and as long as he wishes me to.'

'Is he worth much?'

'I don't know. I've never been interested. Nobody seems to know, anyway. A little, I think. Not enough, I know that. You'd have to ask him.'

'Had the Baroness any money? Of her own?'

'None at all. That's why she married him. She thought *he* had.'

'Please go on.'

'They argued a lot. All the time, in fact. She was always trying to get him interested in some scheme she had. She was always thinking them up. There was the boutique thing. He lost quite a bit on that. Then she started a trout farm. But she didn't know anything about trout and there's already one at Blaine. Then the fish got a disease and died.'

'Did you often see them arguing?'

'Yes.'

'Here?'

'No. She never came here.'

'In the big house?'

'No. In the grounds. Honoré tried to keep it from people. But you could always tell. She flapped her arms about. Like a Frenchwoman. Honoré never did. He was always controlled. More like an Englishman.'

'What about the house? Do *you* think it's worth anything?'

'The pictures might be. And the furniture. There are some folios of drawings, too. Done by the first Baron. He was

76

quite good and they must have some value. They'd raise a little.'

'What about cash? Is there much of that?'

She gave a sad smile. 'Not very much. I don't think he's had a new jacket for years. I knit his jerseys.'

As they left the Baron's cottage, they stood staring at the big house. It was one of the large homes raised by honoured men of Napoleon I's court. It was built of rich mellow stone and had a splendid view over the valley and the road from Brungèges to Lamergelle which crossed the road from Halévé below the house. The grounds at the back were far from extensive and the boundary wall was crowded up against the houses of the village and the church.

But the garden at the front was large and attractive, falling away in its long terraces from the vast box hedge to the road. Originally, it seemed, they had extended across the valley but the Baron's father had sold off a lot of land and had then made more money as a new road to Marcy had been thrust through. It had helped him to stave off the evil day of poverty with which the family were now faced. Unfortunately, the present Baron had no business acumen and virtually nothing left to sell off.

It seemed a good idea to see the village priest. According to Sous-Brigadier Morelot, he was elderly and had known the Baron since he was a boy and would surely know something of the Baroness. He was a shrivelled old man with his grey hair cut *en brosse* and they found him teetering on top of a step-ladder above a small forest of candles before a statue of the Virgin Mary whose halo he was polishing with a rag and brass polish. He climbed down, put away his cloths, then knelt for a moment, his head bowed. As he rose, he smiled. 'A prayer,' he said. 'One day I shall fall off those steps and I always make a point of thanking God that this was not the day.' His smile grew wider. 'Still, it's always better to talk to God than claim He talks to me. When we talk to God it's called praying. When we claim He's talking to us, it's called delusions.'

When they told him about the Baroness's being found, he bobbed his head and his lips moved. '*Requiem aeternam*,' he said. 'I am not surprised.'

'Why not, Father?'

'She was married to a good man but, because he wasn't rich, she couldn't remain faithful to him. However, life isn't supposed to be easy and the Via Crucis is never a path of roses, so we must forgive.'

'Was she a good churchgoer?'

'She tried to be at first. But where she came from they were not Catholics and she soon gave up.'

'Did she come to Confession?'

'At first.'

'Did she tell you anything we should know?'

'Nothing I'm permitted to pass on. The Confession is a closed book.'

'And the Baron?'

'The same applies to him. You ought to know that, my son.'

Pel nodded, accepting the rebuke.

The old priest obviously didn't wish to offer opinions but it was plain enough that, though he had not liked the Baroness, he had never felt anything but warmth for the Baron. Not because he was a particularly good churchgoer, but because he was quite simply a good man who had always accepted his responsibility towards the villagers.

The Baroness, he felt, had made no real attempt to become absorbed in French life or to belong to the village. The only faults he could find in the Baron were his vagueness, his total inability to make a repair satisfactorily, and the wine he served.

'He makes it himself,' he said. 'It looks like the liquid you get when you empty a car radiator. He also produces marc. When he dies the licence will die with him. And perhaps it will be as well. I think you could fuel a blow lamp with it.'

7

The day was warm so they retired for a meal to the bar alongside the garage on the main road. It gave them a splendid view of the ochre-coloured façade of the house, with its half-dozen spear-like cypresses sharp against the deep blue of the sky.

Two men were playing boules on the forecourt of the bar and there was a whiff of Gauloises in the air. But the bar believed in the fashionable new cuisine and the vegetables were hot but not cooked, the meat tasted like old wellington boots, and the wine went down like paint stripper. As they dolefully contemplated the remains of the meal, a car drew in and a man climbed out and approached them. He was burly, red-faced and noisy, and his smile seemed to contain more teeth than he could possibly ever use.

'I'm Emile Jaunay,' he said. 'I'm Maire of this place. I believe you're police.'

Pel left it to Darcy to acknowledge the fact.

'Is it true that the woman who was found at Vieilles Etuves is the Baroness?'

'Nothing's been proved yet,' Darcy said coolly.

'But you think it *is* her?'

'It's possible. Why are you interested?'

Jaunay called for a beer and sat down at their table without asking their leave. 'I'm only interested,' he said, 'because, as Maire, I ought perhaps to call on the Baron. I'm just trying to confirm. I wouldn't like to put my foot in it. I'm a builder and I've done jobs for him – and for her, too – and I knew them pretty well.'

'Did you get paid for the jobs you did?' Darcy asked.

Jaunay gave a nervous laugh. 'I see you've heard about the family finances. Yes, I got paid. They were only small jobs. Repairs. That sort of thing. They were sometimes slow but they always coughed up. They wouldn't have found me willing a second time if they hadn't.'

'Did you know the Baroness well?'

Jaunay flapped his hand in a dismissive gesture. 'A little.'

'Ever see her with another man?'

'Oh, you're on to that one, are you?' Jaunay smiled. 'No, I never did. Though I've heard the story. I heard she'd got one.'

'No idea who it could have been?'

'None at all. Well –' Jaunay sank his beer, 'I'd better be off. Things to do. Thanks for the confirmation. I'll try to see the Baron later. I expect he's pretty low at the moment.'

'I have a suspicion,' Pel remarked,' that it won't make much difference at all to him.'

Jaunay frowned. 'No. Not really,' he said. 'They didn't get on. At least, he'll have some peace now. If you want to know more about the Baroness, try Gilliam. Wyn Spencer Gilliam and his wife. They're English and I think she visited them occasionally.'

Gilliam turned out to be a painter, a tall, handsome ex-British army man who said he had spent a frustrating career in uniform dying to put colour on canvas but never properly able to do so until his retirement. He spoke excellent French and claimed to love France.

'That's why I came here,' he said. 'The quality of light. The only bloody light you get in England's filtered through sheets of rain. My wife found us a place in the Dordogne but, Christ, there's no one there these days but Brits, and I hated the bloody place! I didn't come to France to be surrounded by Brits. Then we got a place in the Tarn. One of those little hill towns. We were all right there for a bite but then the place filled up with yoghurt-weavers.'

Pel's eyes caught Darcy's. 'Yoghurt-weavers?'

Gilliam grinned. 'Well, they didn't weave yoghurt. That would be about as rewarding as trying to nail jelly to a wall. No, they were just a wet lot who seemed to live on lettuce and yoghurt. Health food types who looked on the point of death. They tried to make a living out of what they made. Artificial flowers. Woven cloth which looked like sacking. Nude sculptures that looked as if they'd got a hernia. Paintings that looked as though they'd been done with coloured mud. They didn't know the first thing about light.' He gestured at the canvas he'd been working on. It had style and was ablaze with good Burgundian sunshine, reflecting off the fields, bouncing as if alive from the walls of houses.

'That's what I mean,' Gilliam said. 'It's everywhere in France. If you can't paint that, you should stick to painting doors. They never lasted long, these people who came. A year or so, then they found they'd run out of money, and the French didn't like them, anyway. They used to come and weep on my neck about how unfriendly the French were. In the name of God, you can't be friendly with someone who can only say "Nice weather today", can you?'

It was a familiar refrain and Gilliam seemed to enjoy the fact that it didn't apply to him. 'It never seemed to occur to the silly buggers that they might take a few lessons and spend a few nights learning vocabulary,' he went on. 'Somebody told them that you could learn the language just by living here. Or that all you had to do was shout. Or that all foreigners could speak English.'

Pel was studying a silver salver. It looked valuable but Gilliam didn't seem to regard it with much affection because it was stained and supported a jam jar full of brushes. It carried an inscription: 'Presented to Major the Hon. W.S. Gilliam on his retirement.'

'Hon?' he asked.

'It's a sort of title,' Gilliam explained. 'My father's Lord Marchmont.'

'And you will become Lord Marchmont in time?'

Gilliam grinned and shook his head. 'I doubt it. I have two older brothers both of whom have sons. "Hon." is a sort of consolation prize for younger sons who don't inherit.'

He slashed pale yellow on to his canvas, working with confidence. 'Sell many?' Pel asked.

Gilliam laughed. 'Of course I do. But not here. The locals don't want them. Why should they? They see what I paint every day of their lives – in the flesh, so to speak. I sell a few to tourists who are passing through and want a present for Granny. But this isn't a district where you find many of *them* and, anyway, they don't want to pay the prices I charge. No, I go to England from time to time and take a crateful to a gallery in London that handles my work. Londoners swoon over them. Who wouldn't, if all you see are those bloody awful buildings and all that traffic and the crowds on the Underground. Are *you* interested by the way?'

Pel backed away. He only went in for bargains.

He explained why he was there.

'The Baroness?' Gilliam said. 'I didn't like her. The Baron's not a bad old stick. Bit eccentric but he sometimes drops in for a glass of wine. I prefer that to drinking his, which is ghastly. He gave me permission to paint anywhere in his grounds. I never have. Bit stylized, that sort of subject. But I dropped in. Nice woman, that Marie-Hélène he lived with. Tragic he never married her. Sheer snobbery. But he never had much backbone, I gather. She's far better for him than that silly bitch he did marry.'

'How *did* he come to marry her?'

'Met her at an architectural exhibition. There were photographs of his place on display. I think she was involved with the people who were putting it on.'

'When was it?'

Gilliam smiled. 'I can tell you exactly. Because I visited it. 1976. At the Wesley Hall, Broom Street, London. Put on by Bolt Marketing. It wasn't much of an exhibition. I can't even remember what it was about now. Properties for sale in France or something.'

'Was the Baron's place up for sale at the time?'

'Oh, no. The pictures were just there to get people interested in the region. They got him over to add weight. All expenses paid, of course. Free holiday in London. He'd never have afforded it, otherwise. She could speak some French and was delegated to show him around. There was a bit of a drive on at the time to stir British buyers into buying property in this area. Perhaps you remember it. It didn't seem to come off, because they never sold many. Mind you —' Gilliam grinned, '*I* don't help. Every time I hear of anyone thinking of buying I make a point of meeting them accidentally-on-purpose over a drink and get around to telling them the facts.'

'What facts?'

'That there's no drainage, all the roofs leak, the land's soggy and sour and won't grow anything, and that the water's tainted by ancient cesspits. It usually puts them off.'

Gilliam gave a hoot of laughter. 'I've been known to tell stubborn ones that the area's dotted with plague pits dating back to the Black Death and that the plague's been known to seep through the soil to the surface. I even quote statistics. Not genuine ones. Mine. I found out as a schoolboy that the best way to make room for yourself on a train was to cough a bit and inform everybody around you that you'd just had measles. It always emptied the compartment. But damn it, I came here to get away from Brits so I don't want to be surrounded by the silly buggers, do I? Try Antoine Charrieri.'

'Who's Antoine Charrieri?'

'He's an architect. His offices are in Lyons. In a block he designed himself.'

'Why him?'

'I saw her with him once or twice.'

'Where?'

'Faux-Villecerf. Once when I called on the Baron I saw them together in the yard.'

Looking up Charrieri's number, Pel tried to telephone him. The reply came from an answering machine. 'Sorry, but we are occupied at the moment. Please state your business when the pips go.'

Pel loathed answering machines and he glared at his telephone as though about to bite a lump out of it. At that time of day, Charrieri's office must be functioning, he decided, and the lazy cons were just not bothering.

The message was still being repeated in his ear and he barked into the telephone as the pips finished.

'This is Chief Inspector Pel, of the Brigade Criminelle of the Police Judiciaire. I will now give you an excerpt from my extensive repertoire.' He followed this with a few faltering lines of *Sur le Pont d'Avignon*, then roared at the telephone. 'I now expect to be rung back immediately! I am dealing with murder!'

Not surprisingly, the telephone rang within half an hour and a nervous voice told him that he would be dealt with at any time he cared to arrive. With Darcy still at Faux-Villecerf, he was about to rush out to his car when he decided he had had enough excitement on the road for one day. The eight-wheeled lorry with trailer had unnerved him a little.

He started to yell for his car. When it arrived, Misset was in the driving seat. Pel glared at him. Misset was never Pel's favourite subordinate. He spent too much of his time with his eyes on girls instead of where they should be.

'What are you doing here?' Pel demanded. 'You're supposed to be searching for Feray and Clos.'

'There was nobody else, *patron*,' Misset said.

'Where's Cadet Darras? He could have driven me.'

'On leave, *patron*.'

'Claudie Darel?' Pel enjoyed being driven by Claudie. She looked like a young Mireille Matthieu, and was intelligent and easy to talk to. Unfortunately, they wouldn't have her for much longer because she had just announced her engagement to one of the barristers at the Palais de Justice.

'There's been a breaking and entering at Fontaine,' Misset pointed out. 'Old lady. She's a bit upset, so Claudie went.'

Misset wished he could have gone with Claudie. Her calm was infinitely preferable to Pel's testiness. 'It only left me,' he ended lamely.

Pel climbed into the car. 'Lyons,' he said. 'I'll direct you when we get there.'

Misset let in the clutch and moved forward with Pel watching his every move. He didn't think much of Misset. He was growing fat and lazy. Once upon a time Misset had been in the habit of asking for time off to help with his growing family. Now his family had grown, he didn't bother any more. He would much have preferred it if they could have been fired off into outer space.

For a while they drove in silence. When Pel spoke it made Misset jump.

'Got a line on Feray or Clos yet?' he asked.

'No, *patron*.'

'Nothing?'

'I heard they were back at Tar-le-Petit. I was going there when the call for the car came.'

Pel lit a cigarette without a word. Misset wished *he* could smoke. He would much have preferred to have been going to Tar-le-Petit. He had a date that evening with a woman who worked in a bar near the University and he was praying he would be back in time. He had had it all planned. He'd been intending to do a little gentle questioning at Tar, have a beer or two, then drive back slowly for his date. He wasn't expecting romance but anything was better than going home to his wife. His wife was hardly an agreeable companion at all these days and, in addition, her mother had arrived for a visit. Madame Misset was bad enough; the two of them together were enough to turn milk sour. Even the kids took their side. For that matter, the dog, too. It had once bitten Misset in the ankle for handing out a well-deserved clout to his eldest son.

Charrieri's office occupied the ground floor of a block in the centre of the city near the Pont Bonaparte. It was recognizable at once by its outrageous modernity. The large private car park outside was almost empty but among the modest cars of the office staff was an ostentatious silver Mercedes which somehow seemed to go with a man who could design such a hideous building.

Misset opened the car door for Pel and was just about to sit back and enjoy a cigarette when Pel rounded on him.

'Lock it up,' he said. 'I want you with me.'

'Yes, *patron*,' Misset said meekly. 'I was just coming.'

Charrieri's premises had been designed to impress clients. The main hall was huge. It contained several small shops but to Pel's surprise they were all empty. The staircase to the upper floors was barred by a grill and on the door of the lift was a notice, *Out of Order*.

Despite the signs of disuse in the hall, Charrieri's office looked busy. It was as big as a cathedral and seemed to be entirely walled with glass or orange brick. It was filled with rubber plants and modernistic pottery. On every upright surface were bright water-colours or architect-designed projects — halls, restaurants, leisure centres, shopping malls. After the pattern of all architects' impressions, they were all decorated with trees and as garlanded with flowers as the Vales of Arcadia.

In the front office, behind a small barrier, a young man was sitting before a large drawing board working on plans. Beyond him, at the other side of the barrier, they could see draughtsmen at work with typists and filing clerks. There seemed to be banks of electronic machines that gave Pel nightmares. He hadn't yet even learned to adjust his new digital watch and had to ask Yves Pasquier, aged eleven, from next door, to do it for him.

'What are they all for?' he asked the young man at the drawing board.

'To blind people with science,' the boy said. 'Producing plans. Producing pictures. Calculating measurements. Weights. Stresses. Strains. Costing. There are files, copying machine, computers, electronic typewriters, word processors. All producing enough cost lists and figures to dazzle you. The more paperwork you can push out, the more people are impressed. Especially the big outfits we try to deal with. *They're* blinding people with science themselves, you see, so they understand.' It seemed the young man was something of a cynic.

'How many people work here?' Pel asked.

'You can see them all. They're on display so that clients can see them at point blank range.'

'How many partners?'

'None.'

'You mean all these people are employed here just to keep one man busy?'

'Not all that busy.' The boy gestured at the water-colours round the room. 'He didn't design those. They're just for show. He likes show. He likes to work with two juniors attendant on him, an aide to take down memos and outline his thoughts, and a secretary to hold his hand and keep the world at bay.'

'Does he get that many requests for his time?'

'A few. Here and there. The small jobs he allows his underlings to handle. But the name on the plans, indicating who does them, is always Antoine Charrieri — even if he doesn't.'

Pel eyed the young man for a moment. 'I suspect,' he said drily, 'that you have either been sacked and are serving notice, or else that you expect to be shortly.'

The young man grinned and shrugged. 'I expect to be shortly,' he agreed. 'This isn't my line of country. I suppose you've come to see him.'

'Yes.'

'You'll be lucky. He's not in.'

'He'd better be,' Pel growled.

'However, I heard him say he'd be back. He knows he has an appointment. He blew his top when he heard about it.'

'Does he blow his top often?'

'Regularly.' The boy seemed undisturbed. 'When his debts catch up with him.'

'Does he have many debts?'

'Not more than most people. But he likes to live well so they're big ones, I suppose. He also loses his temper when he finds me drawing faces when I should be drawing plans. He once shoved me off my stool.'

'Did you shove him back?' Pel asked.

The young man grinned. 'He didn't mean anything. He apologized. He's just got a hot temper. He increased my salary to make up for it. I suppose I must be of value to him, though he's not a lot to me. I want to draw people not plans, and one day I will. You'll see my name, Claude Dumanoir, in lights, with Renoir and that lot eventually. But artists don't make a lot of money so I decided to train for this job to tide me over. Bear me in mind.'

Well, it had been an entertaining few minutes and eventually a girl of statuesque proportions, who turned out to be Charrieri's private secretary, ushered them into his inner office. She admitted they were expected but that Charrieri had just slipped out. 'He'll be back,' she said.

'I hope so,' Pel said darkly.

In fact, Charrieri appeared before Pel's notoriously short

fuse had even begun to fizz. He was a tall, handsome man with spectacles hiding enormous eyes, a shock of dark, greying hair, and a high tenor voice. His cheeks were pink and healthy and he looked as if he had disgusting habits like jogging and playing games. He grinned at Pel, unashamed at keeping him waiting.

'I liked your singing, Chief Inspector,' he said cheerfully. 'I must apologize for the over-enthusiasm of my staff, however. My secretary instituted that thing to keep me from being disturbed. It's always answered at once, as you doubtless discovered, but it gives them time to find out from me if I'm involved in some calculations that can't be interrupted. They sometimes go over the top a bit. As you can see, this is a busy office.'

'It's a big one,' Pel admitted. 'But the top floors don't seem to be occupied.'

'They will be.' Charrieri gestured expansively. 'We use one or two rooms for storage, of course. I'm looking for the right people. We don't want noise or anything like that. We need quiet. We've had enquiries but we don't want to fill the lift with office workers or the hall with visitors. We have to consider our own needs –'

Pel decided they could go on all day about Charrieri's office and it was time to get down to business. 'Did you know Bronwen Raby-Labassat?' he asked.

He stared up at the architect with hot eyes. He wasn't very big and Charrieri was handsome, elegant and imposing. But Pel could always make his presence felt when necessary. His question wiped the grin off the architect's face and he seemed to come to attention, almost as if he'd received a barked order.

'Of course I knew her,' he said.

'Do you know anything about her?'

'I suppose so.' ·

'What does that mean?'

'She owes me money.'

'Did you know she was dead?'

'Good God, is she?' Charrieri stepped back, shocked.

'She was found at Vieilles Etuves. She'd been murdered.'

'Good God,' Charrieri said again. 'I read about that. Was it her?'

'Did you know her well?'

'Just as a client. But that's enough to make it a bit of a blow.'

'You met her on more than one occasion?'

'She got me to draw up plans for alterations to the stables at Faux-Villecerf.'

'Altering to what?'

'She wanted a gymnasium.'

'Who for?'

'I assumed for herself. The Baron's a bit old for that sort of thing.'

'And *did* you draw up plans?'

'Yes. Gymnasiums are the thing these days. I belong to one. Don't you?'

Pel ignored the question. Once he left work, he never did anything that might prove painful, difficult or exhausting. 'These plans,' he said. 'Did you draw them up personally?'

'Yes.'

'I understood from the young man in the entrance that you don't normally do trivial jobs of that sort. That you leave them to juniors.'

Charrieri looked down the office at Dumanoir. 'That young man,' he said sharply, 'ought to learn to be a little more discreet. Secrets of that sort aren't to be bandied around. But, yes, I did do the plans myself.'

'A mere conversion from a stable to a gymnasium?'

'It was to be quite a gymnasium. In addition, of course, the lady was a baroness. Doing work for a baroness can be quite a cachet. I thought it might be useful publicity. Unfortunately it seems to have turned out somewhat differently.'

'Were you going to put money into this gymnasium?'
Charrieri's eyebrows shot up. 'Not likely.'

'Do you ever put money into the projects you design?'

'No, thank you.' Charrieri's answer was brisk. 'Speculation's a risky game. You have to be sure you're onto a good thing.'

'Why did she come to you?' Pel gestured round the office. 'I imagine your fees are high and for an alteration from a stable to a gymnasium she could just as easily have gone to an architectural draughtsman. There are plenty who do that sort of thing, I believe. People well able to draw up simple plans for a builder to work from. Perhaps some of your staff do.'

'I'm sure they do.'

'They'd come a lot cheaper than you, I imagine.'

'I'm sure they would. Even Dumanoir could do it. I believe he does occasionally — for things like garden sheds.'

The comment drew a sour look from the body at the drawing board.

Pel glanced from one to the other. 'So why you?' he asked.

'I can only think,' Charrieri said, 'it was because she hadn't heard of Dumanoir.'

'Were you happy with the arrangement?'

Charrieri looked puzzled and Pel explained. 'If your fees are high, wouldn't you make sure before you did any work that the prospective client could pay? She sounds to me as if she might have been a doubtful starter and I imagine you don't draw up expensive plans without making sure the money's available.'

Charrieri shrugged. 'That's true, of course. We usually make a few discreet enquiries. But the work involved in this project was small and she made sure I understood the money *was* available.'

'But I gather the Baron is virtually penniless. All he's got is a large property with a garden, a little land, a view, and not much else.'

'That's what I discovered. But when I pointed this out she insisted she *had* money. Her own money, she said.'

'Didn't you think a gymnasium a strange project for a family everybody felt was penniless?'

'I might have done if she hadn't been so insistent that *she* wasn't.'

'The family insist they have no money at all. So where did this money she says she had come from?'

Charrieri shrugged. 'When we make enquiries, we don't go that far,' he admitted. 'You do have to take a little on trust. But I did make it clear to her that we're expensive. She still continued to insist that all bills would be met.' He paused. 'Under the circumstances,' he ended, frowning, 'I have a feeling they won't.'

Pel nodded. 'Not by her, they won't,' he agreed.

They got little else from Charrieri but they did receive a sidelong comment from the boy near the entrance as they left.

'Don't let him kid you,' he said quietly. 'Of course he speculates. A lot do if it looks good.'

Pel gestured at the office. 'Such as this?'

The boy grinned.

'Did he go in for this gymnasium project?'

Dumanoir smiled. 'Shouldn't think so. You wouldn't get much out of a gymnasium in the middle of nowhere, would you?'

8

'No question about it any more,' Darcy reported. 'She's exactly who we decided she was. Bronwen Raby-Labassat, née Davis, of Barry, near Cardiff in South Wales. Parents dead. The British police produced a dental report on her.' Darcy looked pleased with himself. 'I tried London first but, in view of her name, they suggested trying Cardiff. They found her straight away. They even knew her. She'd been a beauty queen before she started working for that outfit in London where the Baron met her. She even got her name in the paper when she married him. You know the stuff. *Local Girl Marries French Nobleman*. Sarrazin would have approved.'

'You haven't had a written confession sent by post by her murderer, I suppose?' Pel asked drily.

Darcy ignored the sarcasm. 'We searched her drawers and cupboards. Nothing of note. Nothing to indicate what she was doing at Vieilles Etuves. Just a paper with directions in her writing on it.'

'Directions for what?'

'A route. But not to Vieilles Etuves.' Darcy pushed a small piece of paper at Pel. It read 'N74 to N6. N6 to Macon. Motorway to Bourg and Nantua. Road runs alongside Swiss border to lake.'

'That seems to make it directions to Geneva or Evian-les-Bains. South side of Lac Léman. What's her interest there?'

'I went to see if the Baron knew. He wasn't in. Marie-Hélène Gaussac produced a bit more about her, though. On one of her trips into the blue, she went off with the key to that small door near the steps they use. She sent it back in an envelope post-marked St-Flô. That's on Lac Léman. I asked among the family and learned that she's also visited Aix-les-Bains, Montperreux near Pontarlier, Annécy and Maisod. Nobody knew why.'

'What's so special about them?'

'Well, for one thing, they're all on the edge of a lake.' Darcy pushed a map of France forward and his finger jabbed at the areas of blue among the green.

Pel frowned. 'Antoine Charrieri talked about her having access to money,' he said. 'Have we checked her bank?'

'Yes, *patron*, we have. You know how cagey they are but I leaned on them. There are three payments to her of 10,000 francs unexplained. All in the last three months. That must be the money she meant. Where did it come from? It didn't come from the Baron. He's as poor as a church mouse and the bank admitted that he hadn't got that much.'

'Pay?' Pel suggested. 'Was she a high-class *horizontale*?'

'Ten thousand is a lot of money for that, *patron*.'

'She was involved in some sort of deal to change the stable block at the chateau to a gymnasium. God knows what she expected from it. Let's see if there's anything else. If there was, it must have gone through the Maire's office.'

Sure enough, plans concerning the chateau had been deposited in Jaunay's official office. But they referred only to the cottage in the grounds where the Baron lived and indicated the alterations he wished to make. They also showed a second cottage, however – the one on the slopes below the chateau that contained the barn and cow byre atop the high wall overlooking the road.

'Whose is that?'

'It belongs to the Baron,' Jaunay said. 'Josephe Sully lives there.'

'Who's Josephe Sully?'

'He was a small farmer. Retired now. He had a little land on the hill up to Quétigny and kept a few cows. He always brought them down for the winter and kept them in the byre alongside the cottage.'

'What's intended there?'

'The Baroness had plans to develop it. She wanted to modernize it. I think she wanted to let it. To holiday-makers. It was one of her plans for making money. We all knew of them. They were always popping up. None were very practical.'

It seemed to be time to see the Baron again. His pale eyes blank and uninterested, the old man shrugged when faced with the questions and barely looked up from the plank he was sawing. In the end they managed to draw him away and he even offered them wine. The general opinion about it appeared to be well justified. It was vaguely orange in colour and tasted like sludge. The Baron knocked back his own glass without blinking but they noticed Marie-Hélène Gaussac refrained from drinking.

'This project of the Baroness's over the stable block?' Pel asked. 'What was she trying to do, do you think?'

The Baron shrugged. 'Make money, I expect,' he said. 'She was always trying to think of ways of doing that. Chiefly because we never had much. We have the chateau, of course, but that eats it, it doesn't make it.'

'She'd been to an aerobic studio in Dijon,' Marie-Hélène interrupted and the Baron nodded. 'She went regularly. Perhaps she thought she could set up something of the sort here?'

'In Faux-Villecerf? It's miles from anywhere. Who'd come?'

The Baron shrugged again.

'What about the cottage? The one by the road.'

'She wanted to make it earn money. But old Sully's lived there all his life. His father was living there when I was a boy. I'm not going to throw him out.'

'Would your wife have?'

'She'd have tried.'

'And *this* cottage. Your cottage. It's shown in the plan in the Maire's office. What were you intending?'

'I was going to repair the roof. Perhaps an extra room. That's all. I enjoy living here.'

'Don't you like the big house?'

'No. But it's my duty to preserve it for my son when his time comes.'

Pel had seen the Baron's do-it-yourself efforts. They hadn't improved anything much. 'So you moved out?' he said.

'Yes. With Marie-Hélène. She's always looked after me. We were always — comfortable — yes, comfortable — together. I set her up in an apartment in town when I was pushed into marriage. Soon afterwards she married, too. We tried to play fair, you see. Then Marie-Hélène lost her husband and when it became clear my wife was ill and wouldn't recover we started again.'

'What about your second wife?'

The Baron looked puzzled. 'I suppose I married her because I thought she had money and that it would save the estate.' He gave a wheezy laugh and Pel caught a blast of bad breath. 'She thought *I* had money.'

'And Marie-Hélène?'

'She stepped aside again. She's a noble person. I returned to her when I found my wife had male friends. My wife didn't worry. She was a small-town woman and it pleased her to have a title. She was always going into things with other people's money. She opened a boutique in the city with money put up by a Thomas Legendre, a man she'd met. It didn't work. She knew nothing about buying and selling clothes and neither did he. I suspect the gymnasium was something of the same sort.'

'Whose was *that* money?'

The old man didn't bother to answer. He seemed to have lost interest and merely shrugged.

It seemed to be time to try to find out about the Raby-Labassats from some source other than themselves.

For some time Pel debated how to go about it and in the end came up with the name of Baron de Mougy. De Mougy and Pel were old friends and old enemies. Pel had recovered jewellery his wife had had stolen and had consulted him in the case of a murder when the victim had been a German they'd believed to be an SS officer who had terrorized the district during the war.

As a young man De Mougy had been one of the leaders of the Resistance and he had known everything worth knowing about every man and woman under his command. Pel had a feeling he would also know everything there was to know about the aristocracy of the region. He was clever and didn't miss much that went on.

He was a tall man with a face like a hatchet, handsome but ice-cold. He didn't like Pel any more than Pel liked him but they had a wholesome respect for each other and, at least, his wine was worth drinking. He wasn't mean with it either. The bottle that was brought out – not by the Baron but by a manservant – had a label that made Pel's hair stand on end at what it must have cost.

'Raby-Labassat,' Pel said.

De Mougy looked up. 'Know him,' he said. 'Decayed place at Faux-Villecerf. Old family. No backbone.'

There was one thing about De Mougy. He didn't waste words. And 'No backbone' was never something that could ever have been said about him. He was growing old now but he was still as hard as iron. And despite being on the run from the Germans for most of the war, he had somehow never once allowed his own splendid chateau to become run-down. De Mougy was a survivor. Raby-Labassat was a born victim.

'Know anything about him?' Pel asked.

'Understand he's having a bit of trouble at the moment.'

Well, if a murdered wife was a bit of trouble, then, yes, Raby-Labassat *was* having a bit of trouble.

'Ever meet his wife?'

'Yes. Damn fool.'

De Mougy's wife wasn't a damn fool. She was younger than De Mougy, beautiful and clever, and it was rumoured De Mougy had acquired her by rescuing her father from bankruptcy.

'Is there money?' Pel asked.

'None at all.'

'How do you know?'

'I've tasted his wine.'

It seemed a good enough reason.

'There must have been money once.'

'There's none now.' De Mougy gave Pel a hard look. It was like being skewered with a rapier. 'He once asked me if it would cost much to have his place renovated. If you have to ask how much a thing like that costs, then obviously you can't afford it. They didn't keep an eye on their money. It pays to keep an eye on your money. They put theirs into the wrong things. They even tried to get away with their taxes. They thought the government wouldn't notice. But they did. They have ways of finding out. Property's the thing. Property's the only thing that increases in value. So long, of course, as it has the approval of the government. France's riddled with bureaucracy and you can't get anywhere without it.'

'What about the children? Have you met them?'

'Half-wits. One of them plays in a band. The daughter's a Marxist lunatic. Only one of them with a worthwhile job. And he's not much to write home about. My son's got a degree in agronomy ready for when he takes over the estate from me.'

Darcy turned up Thomas Legendre, the man who had gone into the clothing business with the Baroness. He was a small effeminate man she had met in a bar. His mother had just died and, having inherited a little money, he had hoped to invest it in something profitable. He had listened to the Baroness's arguments and gone into the boutique business with enthusiasm. Instead of making a fortune, he had lost his inheritance and was now working in the toy department of the Nouvelles Galéries in Dijon.

'I thought I could trust her,' he said. 'She was full of ideas and said she knew all about it. But she didn't know what to order or how to order or when to order.'

No wonder, Pel thought, that clothing shops turned out to be full of flimsy summer fashions while it was still hurling down sleet and snow in early spring, and thick autumn fashions with tweeds and heavy collars as the summer reached its peak in a heat wave.

It was obvious Thomas Legendre wasn't a suspect.

They didn't seem to be moving forward very fast but then they had an unexpected stroke of luck. The cops at Faux-Villecerf were still keeping their ears and eyes open as instructed and were passing along small titbits of infor-mation, none of which were of much help, until Morelot, the sous-brigadier, remembered picking up a man called Arnaud just before the Baroness had disappeared. He had bumped into him almost accidentally late at night on the edge of the Baron's land. He had immediately assumed he was doing a bit of poaching. There was game on the few remaining hectares belonging to the Raby-Labassats and it was not unknown for one or two of the shiftier inhabitants of Faux-Villecerf to remove them occasionally. Arnaud had appeared before the magistrates on a charge of trespassing.

'Actually,' Morelot told Darcy, 'I might just have ticked him off and sent him home, because the Baron couldn't care less who walks across his land. But he used lip to me and he's a nasty piece of work, anyway – up to all sorts of things. So I thought I'd teach him a lesson. You have to do it now and then to keep the place in some sort of order.'

Darcy knew the feeling. He'd been a uniformed cop on the streets himself once. 'I found him among the trees,' Morelot continued. 'He said he was hiding because the Baroness was about. At two o'clock in the morning? I thought he was just making excuses and ran him in. But now the Baroness's dead I wondered and asked him again about it. He says he heard her voice and saw a car parked among the trees and thought she was in it with one of her boy-friends. I thought I'd better pass it on.'

'It was a good idea. Let's go and see this Arnaud.'

Arnaud was working in the garden at the back of his house. It was a small dwelling at the end of the village street, built of the local stone.

'Alardie Arnaud,' Darcy said. 'We know you well.' He'd taken the trouble to check with Records.

Arnaud looked like a dog threatened with a bath. He was a small man with a cap that clung to the back of his head as though it were nailed there. 'That's over,' he growled.

'Not necessarily. You were recently picked up in the early hours of the morning on the Baron's land.'

'I admitted it. I hadn't much choice.'

'What were you after?'

'Cement.'

The reply startled Darcy. A pheasant, a chicken – that would have been normal enough. But cement! 'Cement?' he said. 'Are you sure?'

'Of course I'm sure.'

'Why cement?'

'To build a bit on the back of my house.' Arnaud gestured and, turning, Darcy saw he had built a wall and was on the

101

point of installing a door frame. 'The Baron was doing it, so why not me? I thought I'd build a kitchen and bathroom and make the present kitchen a bedroom and make the living-room bigger. We nearly sit on each other's knees to watch *Dallas*.'

Darcy studied him. 'This cement: Did you know of some you were going to pinch?'

'Yes.'

'*Did* you pinch it?'

'No. That idiot, Morelot, came along.'

Darcy paused. 'Did you know where there was a store of it or something?' he asked.

'Yes. He'd got a lot.'

'Who had?'

'The Baron. He had it stacked away.'

'And it was while you were prowling around after it that you ran into Sous-Brigadier Morelot?'

'No. He ran into me.'

'Why were you hiding when he found you?'

'I saw this car.'

'Which car?'

'It was black. Tucked away among the trees.'

'What sort was it?'

'I don't know. I couldn't see.'

'Big?'

'No. Little.'

'When exactly was this?'

'Just about the time the Baroness disappeared. A few days before, I think.'

'Did you see anyone with this car?'

'One was a woman. I supposed it was the Baroness because it was on their land. I decided she was with one of her boy-friends. She had one or two.'

'Did you hear them saying anything?'

'I just heard the Baroness say something about "I prefer it with water." I thought they'd got a bottle in there. Then I sloped off and bumped into Morelot.'

'Where was this cement you found out about?'

'In what used to be the pump house. It was once used to lift water from the river up to the house. It's used as a store now. There were around two hundred bags. I didn't think they'd miss a couple.'

'Is it still there?'

'Nobody's moved it.'

The cement was there all right but enquiries showed that nobody knew anything about it.

'It's not mine,' the Baron insisted. 'Though, since it's there I'll probably use some of it. I ordered ten bags. Somebody must have got it wrong, and it must have been my wife who had it put in the pump house. I thought it hadn't come and was going to reorder.'

Since the Baroness was no longer around to ask, Darcy took his question to the Baron's sons and daughter. They also knew nothing.

'I expect the old fool was going to waste our money doing up that old pile of rubbish,' Philomène said.

The only way to find out, it seemed, was to ask the manufacturers whose name was on the bags.

'Two hundred bags of cement,' Darcy said. 'Supplied to the Chateau of Faux-Villecerf.'

'We don't supply to individual buyers,' the manufacturers told him. 'Only to builders' merchants.'

That involved another set of questions until Darcy found the builders' merchant who had supplied the cement.

'Ten bags were ordered,' they said. 'We advertised it cheap. It was from a building project near Arles that fell through. Then the Baron increased the order.'

'He says he didn't.'

'Well, it was somebody who said he was the Baron. I took the order myself. On the telephone.'

'Who paid?'

'So far, no one. And, considering we've billed them several times and received no reply, it seems nobody's going to.'

9

It seemed a good idea to see Emile Journay, the Maire. Since he was a builder, he might just know who had ordered the cement. It was obviously intended for some sizeable project somewhere in the area.

As soon as he mentioned the subject, Darcy knew he had struck gold. Jaunay looked uncomfortable.

'Yes,' he admitted. 'I was the one who increased the order.'

'Why?'

'The Baroness asked me to.'

'Was she going to pay for it?'

'She said so.'

'Where was the money coming from?'

'Some type was going to advance it.'

'Why didn't she pay?'

Jaunay's face twisted. 'I don't know. She changed her mind about the project, I think.'

'What project was it?'

'It had something to do with the stables. She was talking of building a gymnasium.'

'We've heard of that. But at Faux-Villecerf? Why? And what about this type who was going to advance the money? What was his interest?'

'I don't know. Bronwen said it was all right to go ahead.'

'You called her "Bronwen". Did you know her well?'

'Well, we all knew each other, didn't we? Those of us who had a bit of – well,' Jaunay gestured, 'you know, a bit more money than the rest.'

'The Baroness hadn't any money. Did you buy anything else for her?'

'Bricks. Breeze blocks. The price's rising. It seemed a good idea. They've been stacked at Dole for some time.'

'Timber? Window frames? Doors? Tiles? Plaster? That sort of thing?'

'Yes.'

'Cheap stuff?'

'Some of it was old.'

'How much was there altogether?'

'A lot.'

'Did she pay for that?'

'Yes, she did for that.'

'What with?'

Journay shrugged. His answers seemed to come reluctantly from him. 'I admit I was worried at the amount being spent. But I was told to get on with it. I was used because I was a builder and knew how to order. I also got discount.'

'Were *you* going to do the building?'

'I hoped so.'

'Wasn't whoever was pushing this thing over-ordering a bit – for a gymnasium? It wouldn't involve all that much rebuilding, would it? Wouldn't it mostly be just tidying up? Reflooring. Plastering. A new roof. Some heating.'

'I suppose so. But there seemed to be a lot of money in it and I wasn't paying. I was just expecting to get the contract for the building.'

'Would it have been all *that* profitable? For the conversion of a stable?'

Jaunay looked uncomfortable. 'I thought there must be something bigger in the background. All those bricks and so on. But I didn't know what.'

'And you didn't enquire too deeply because, if there were

something bigger – you'd have done well out of it. Was it a promise?'

'I suppose so.'

'Not a contract?'

'No.'

'But you were prepared to go into it – even if it was on the cheap and a bit dubious – for what you'd get out of it.'

Jaunay frowned. 'I'm in business. I employ a lot of men. A builder can't afford to have his men idle. He's always got to be looking for new openings. And big projects mean work over a long period.'

'The Baroness – did you know her perhaps a little better than you've so far suggested?'

Jaunay flushed. 'Keep your voice down. My wife's around.'

'These boy-friends the Baroness is said to have had. Were you one?'

'I was once.'

'What colour's your car?'

'Yellow. It's a Peugeot. I bought a yellow one because you get mists around here in winter and yellow's the best colour there is for being seen when visibility's bad.'

'Have you a black car?'

'My wife has.'

'Were you using it one night in the grounds of the chateau?'

'I've never been in the grounds of the chateau in my wife's car. I always use the Peugeot.'

'Were you still the Baroness's boy-friend?'

'No. I found out she'd got someone else.'

'Anyone you knew?'

Jaunay frowned. 'No. I thought it would be –' he stopped dead.

'Well, come on,' Darcy urged. 'Who? Someone from round here?'

Jaunay looked like a small boy robbed of a toy. 'I thought

it would be that English con, Gilliam.'

'Why do you call him that?'

Jaunay looked shifty. 'You need to look pretty carefully at Gilliam,' he said. 'He's a — what do they call them? — a remittance man. He *had* to come and live in France. Don't be taken in by all that stuff about wanting to paint. He was mixed up in something shady. Money was involved, I heard.'

'Who told you this?'

'The Baroness.'

'How did *she* learn the story?'

'I'll give you three guesses.'

Major Gilliam was sitting in his garden in front of an easel when Pel and Darcy appeared. His wife was just leaving. She gave them an icy stare and climbed into her car to drive off with spinning wheels and a savage swerve at the corner.

'Somebody's in a bad temper,' Pel murmured.

'Somebody else's probably in a bad temper, too,' Darcy commented. 'She's got what looks like a bruise on her face.'

Gilliam welcomed them cheerfully enough and brought out a bottle of wine.

'We passed your wife on the way out,' Pel said. 'She didn't seem very pleased to see us.'

'Holy Mother of God,' Gilliam said. 'Did she say anything?'

'She did a bit of looking.'

'I expect you saw the black eye I gave her.'

'Is that what it was?'

'Unintended. She went on and on at me. About her not having any friends. And about moving back to the Dordogne where they all speak English and you go for drinks and get dressed up and generally behave as if you lived in Cheltenham.'

'There is something special about this Cheltenham?'

'It's where they behave like that. My wife's sort, anyway. Because I'm an "Hon." and a major, they expect me to behave like that too. My wife loved it. When we were living in the Dordogne she thought she was living the life of Riley. All her friends were Brits. But she was really bored out of her mind. When she started on again about it I lost my temper.'

'You've got a temper?'

'Haven't you? It was intended to be a push but she ducked and got it in her eye. I shouldn't have done it. But I did. It's not the happiest of marriages, I suppose.'

There seemed to be a lot of them about, Pel decided. He took a look at what Gilliam was working on. It was an oil showing the valley in front of the chateau at Faux-Villecerf. It was surprisingly good and even Pel, who was far from being an expert, recognized the fact. It had an extraordinary quality of light and showed the glow of the sun in the way only Burgundians knew.

'*Pas mal*,' he said.

'No,' Gilliam agreed. 'Not bad. It'll sell in London. We have something here that people long for in London. Sunshine. They don't get a lot of it and they're prepared to pay good money for it. That's why I splash on the white and the primrose yellow and paint the skies a deeper blue than they are. Colour's priceless to people in Britain.'

Pel let him go on a little before he stopped him dead in his tracks. 'How well did you know the Baroness?' he asked quietly.

'Hardly at all.'

'For a man who knew her hardly at all, you supplied us with a surprising amount of information about her. Do you still say you hardly knew her?'

'Yes.'

'How did you know so much about her then? Did *she* tell you?'

'Well, yes, I suppose so.'

'Were you a *friend* of the Baroness?'

Gilliam laughed. 'Of course. She loved her title and always used it. And because my father had one she thought we belonged to the same set. I never belonged to my set, of course, and with two older brothers I'm never likely to. But it pleased her to think we both belonged to some sort of élitist club.'

Pel paused, then he tossed his next question abruptly at Gilliam. 'Why did you come to France, Major Gilliam?' he asked. 'I understand it wasn't just because you wanted to paint French sunlight.'

Gilliam's face darkened and his eyes glittered with anger. 'So you've heard that story, have you? he said. 'Who told you that? That thick-headed bastard, Jaunay?'

'Is what I heard correct? I heard you were mixed up in something shady, that money was involved.'

Gilliam's smile returned. 'It sounds like Jaunay. Still, it doesn't matter. It was too long ago. No, Chief, it wasn't money. It was a woman. Another officer's wife. That's why I retired from the army. Like a fool, I told the story to Bronwen.'

'*Why* did you tell her? Were you ever *more* than just friends?'

Gilliam paused with his glass in his hand, then he hoisted it to his lips and emptied it. 'You *are* persistent, aren't you?'

'This is a murder enquiry.'

'Well, you know what she was like. And my wife's become a bloody bore. Yes, we were like that.'

'Lovers?'

'I slipped once or twice. But I decided, as I did the other time, that I was getting into deep waters and I'd better get ashore damn quick.'

'Did your wife find out about you?'

'Perhaps. Perhaps that's why she goes to the Dordogne so much. That's where she's gone now.'

'You speak good French.'

'German, too. In my family, it was considered a good

110

investment in case one of the sons decided for diplomacy. I lived in France for a year as a youth. With a titled family, of course. Nothing else would do. They were like the Baron. They had a fine house and no money and, rather than work, they took in paying guests.'

Pel decided that Gilliam was clever and more than just a man with a desire to paint pictures. 'What was the Baroness up to?' he asked.

'God knows. She talked of making the chateau into a motel or something.'

'That place?'

'With money spent on it, it could be.'

'She hadn't got any money.'

'Gilliam gestured with his brush. A spot of yellow paint landed on Pel's shoe. Pel stared at it. Gilliam didn't apologize but he wiped it off with his handkerchief. 'That's what banks are for, isn't it?' he said. 'If she'd put up a good case, she'd have got a loan.'

'Could she have handled it?'

'I doubt it.'

'You interested in any of her projects?'

'I once lent her two or three thousand francs to start a bar in Halève. It was redecorated but then she found she'd have to do the serving herself and it never came to anything.'

'What about the hotel idea?'

'She asked if I'd go in with her. I said no thank you. My wife's family made their money from hotels. They had a string of them. And my father has a big house in Hampshire. He has to have daily visitors at five pounds a time to raise money to stop the roof leaking. Lots of his friends are at it. But the roofs never get better and the furniture and the fittings always get worse.'

There was still one other person they hadn't yet seen — Josephe Sully, the retired farmer who lived in the cottage by the main road on the edge of the Baron's land, in the house the Baroness had considered making into a holiday home.

He was in his late seventies, a dim old man living alone. His cottage — the one with the cow byre over the road — was a ramshackle affair shored up at the back with timber.

He wore thick glasses with a twisted frame and a cracked lens. His face was covered with scraps of sticking plaster of various shades and cleanliness, as though some had been there a long time while others were of more recent attachment.

'Cut myself shaving,' he explained. 'Often do. Often. Often. Don't see so well.'

He repeated everything he said. He was deaf as well as short-sighted and wanted to make sure they heard him properly.

He gestured round his cottage. 'Falling down,' he pointed out. 'Down. They never gave me a pension, you see. Never. Never. They couldn't afford to. But the Baron said I could live in the cottage. He said I could. I liked that. It suited my plans.'

He bent to stroke an old dog sleeping by his feet. It looked as if it had been knitted from dirty white wool and smelled as if it had been simmering for a while in a saucepan with bones. Pel kept his head averted as he spoke.

'These plans of yours,' he said. 'Were you wanting to do the place up?'

'Couldn't afford to,' Sully said. 'Hadn't got the money.'

'What were the plans then?'

'Dying. Dying. That's all. Just dying.'

'*You were planning to die?*' The thought of death was anathema to Pel. He always considered he was already too near to it for comfort and preferred not to talk about it.

The old man was nodding. 'Yes,' he said. 'Here. I want to die here. In this cottage. She said I had to get out. But I had nowhere to go and the Baron said I didn't have to. He said so.'

'But the Baroness said you should?'

'She said so. She did. She did. I'd just got used to the idea when she disappeared.'

'*Why* did she want you to leave?'

'I heard she wanted to use the cottage to earn money. But I don't know. I don't. It's no good as a cottage. Nobody will want it. No one. Never.'

'Had she plans for it?'

'She wanted to do it up and let it. To holiday-makers. She couldn't do that. She couldn't. It only remained standing because I was always putting things right.'

'What rent did you pay?'

'I didn't pay any rent. Never.'

'Which meant that she could chuck you out at any time.'

'She couldn't have done it. My relations would never have let her. I've got a few around somewhere. And the Baron wouldn't have let her. He wouldn't. I've known him since he was a boy. He said I wouldn't have to go. He always said so.'

10

The newspapers continued to dwell on the death of the Baroness Raby-Labassat for a time but then she disappeared in one fell swoop from the front pages. A Welshwoman married to an impoverished baron didn't stand a chance against the Queen of England who was on a visit to the President of the Republic. Having got rid of their own royal family, the French had always shown a remarkable enthusiasm for their British counterparts and Bronwen disappeared abruptly from the public consciousness.

Pel studied the local paper with some relief. It was always easier to work without comments from the press. Laying the paper down, he set about the files on his desk. It seemed he could tick off Brochard's sheep poisoning. Brochard had reported it well and truly wrapped up.

'It wasn't hard,' he said. 'Not for a type like me who was raised on a farm. I opened up one of the dead sheep. Its stomach contained yew leaves. Sheep don't go for yew leaves.'

'They don't? So how did they get there?'

'Sloppy husbandry, *patron*. Barthelot had been allowing his sheep to eat them. And yews are poisonous. Both the bark and the leaves. Cattle and sheep graze round yew trees without ill effect but it's far from unknown for farm stock to be poisoned by eating yew clippings. I think they know instinctively that the tree's poisonous but they eat the clippings if they come across them mixed in with other feed.'

Brochard explained what had happened. 'To make matters worse,' he said, 'he'd stacked bags of chemical fertilizer in the wrong place and some were split. I know the stuff. It would knock over an elephant. I reckon he's actually been feeding the clippings and fertilizer himself to his animals by accident for ages. No wonder the sheep died. He was even poisoning his daughter's horse with it. We could probably charge him with making fraudulent claims against the Guillemard Assurance Company. He claimed his ewes were prize Larzacs but they're nothing of the sort. And they're all suffering from braxy.'

'What in God's name is braxy?'

'A sort of gastro-enteritis, usually caused by bad farming methods.'

Pel studied Brochard's smooth face, impressed.

'I've passed all the information to the insurance company,' Brochard ended. 'I expect they'll want to talk to him. I marked the report "No action necessary".'

Pel stared after him as the door slammed.

'As I said,' he remarked slowly to Darcy, 'that young man has hidden depths.'

Having sorted out the business of the poisoned ewes to his satisfaction, Brochard completed the paperwork and sat back. It was late and he was in need of a drink. He decided on the Bar du Destin. Charlie Ciasca would be there. Their meetings had been going on at intervals all through the business with Barthelot's sheep.

The bar was full and a football match on the television was claiming the rapt attention of most of the customers. Charlie Ciasca was studying the drawings in her sketching pad. She was a very busy girl and so far all their meetings had been rushed, so that Brochard had not got very far.

115

'When are we really going to get together?' he asked.

'What do you mean?'

'There are always hundreds of other females around when I call at your flat.'

'Hundreds?'

'Well, several. Why can't we be alone sometimes?'

'Where?'

'We could go away for a weekend.'

She grinned. 'My brothers would be on to you like a couple of thunderbolts.'

'What have they got against me?'

'They protect me.'

'What from?'

'Men like you. They once beat up a man for molesting me.'

'Why?'

'I don't go in for that sort of thing.'

'You don't?'

'Well, I'm not fanatic about it, but they are.'

'Are they tough?'

'They have bolts sticking out of their necks. Like Frankenstein.'

'What do they do for a living? Are they night-club bouncers?'

'No. They run a boat on Lake Geneva.'

'You mean Lac Léman.'

'I mean Lake Geneva. I told you: I'm part Swiss and the Swiss call it Lake Geneva.'

'What do they use the boat for? Fishing?'

'The fishing's not all that good. They do trips. For tourists.'

It seemed that, with an Italian capacity for disaster, Papa Ciasca's business was always teetering on the brink of collapse and the family were heavily dependent on the ancient boat his sons, Jean-Jacques and Gabriel, plied for holiday-makers. During the day it was used for trips about

116

the lake and at night to haul tourists from the Swiss side of the lake where, with good Swiss thrift, the casino limits were low, to the French side where they were considerably more generous.

'It's one of those things like a small *bateau mouche*,' Charlie explained. 'It's covered with glass with twenty rows of seats. Forty francs round the lake. No wind. No spray on your face. You think you're a sailor but it's like being in a floating conservatory.'

'Do they make much money?'

She gave him an odd look. 'Not at that, they don't,' she said.

As Brochard had left, Pel had sat back. It was always satisfying to see a case wrapped up. It was a perpetual war, and each little case was a campaign.

Nosjean's garage at Genois with its list of hot cars had also been terminated and reached the paperwork stage.

'Will you pull it off?' Pel asked.

'Judge Castéou thinks so,' Nosjean said. So do I. Mind you, I think Giraud, the type who owned the place, wasn't in it on his own. I asked him and he swore no one else was. But I think he just didn't have the courage to say so. So he carries the can.'

'Why do you think someone was pushing him?'

'Because he's not talking and the solicitor who's representing him is Dugusse. I expect you remember *him*, *patron*.'

'I remember him. He was the late Maurice Tagliatti's mouthpiece.'*

'And Maurice was a gangster. I reckon Dugusse has been put up by whoever's leaning on Giraud. He'll make sure Giraud goes down. To put him out of the way. So nobody

* See *Pel And The Picture of Innocence*

talks to him. So that whoever's behind him will be able to fold up the operation. So nobody will dig any deeper.'

'And who do you think *was* behind it?'

'Maurice Tagliatti's old outfit. That's why Dugusse is in it.'

'What we left of Maurice's old lot transferred their allegiance to Carmen Vlaxi.'

'That's right, *patron.*'

With Nosjean's case tidied up, apart from the Baroness Raby-Labassat there was only Orega and the gang who had relieved Merciers' of their trays of rings. They were due to appear before the magistrates and the chances were that they would cease to trouble the police for a while.

Pel frowned. By this time he was certain that Orega's little affair had also been backed by Carmen Vlaxi. Orega was a hit and rush type with not much finesse. His fingerprints had been all over the glass top of the jewellers' counter and in the stolen car they had used. But there was one man still free – the fifth man Nosjean and De Troq' had noticed – and he surely fitted in somewhere.

Pel didn't like things to be incomplete. Was this fifth man the liaison between Orega and whoever was behind him? Either way he must be a crook.

But who was he? They still didn't know.

The Bar Transvaal behind the Hôtel de Police was crowded. Among the customers were a number of cops because it was a handy place to get a beer and sandwich when there was no time to take lunch. Pel had often eaten breakfast there in the days before his marriage, when Madame Routy's shellac-tasting coffee had revolted him. His beer seemed to lie heavy on his stomach and he wondered if he had an ulcer coming on.

'Bronwen,' he said to Darcy. 'Who do you put your money on?'

They had investigated old Sully's relations and come up with nothing. Most of them lived up near the Belgian border and hadn't heard of the murder. They hadn't even been aware that the old man was still alive. Of course, in village communities, there were always probably a few loose ends somewhere that nobody knew about and Faux-Villecerf might well be full of aunts, uncles, nephews and nieces who could find in the old boy's precarious circumstances good reason for a grudge against the Baroness.

Darcy didn't think so, however. 'It doesn't make sense,' he argued. 'If it had been the Baron who died it would have been straightforward. His family all want to get their hands on his property. One because he thinks that as the next baron it's his right. Another because he feels the house is draining away the family fortune. The daughter because she's in debt to the tune of 20,000 francs. I checked and she is. It comes to the same thing in the end with all of them. Greed.'

There was no point in worrying about alibis. Too much time had elapsed and Minet and Cham couldn't agree on when Bronwen had died. They knew she'd been missing for six weeks and four days but she could have been killed at any time during that period.

'And this cash she told Charrieri she had,' Pel said. 'Where was it coming from?' His mind was prowling about like a caged leopard, frustrated, angry. Real life police work was never like the stuff you saw on television. It didn't consist of intuitive flashes and violent chases. It involved checking and re-checking and that was sometimes as exciting as watching grass grow.

There was something wrong with the whole case, he decided. They even had the wrong victim, he felt. If it had been the Baron who was dead, he might have understood and looked more deeply into his family. But the Baroness could be dead for an entirely different reason. Because, for instance, one of her boy-friends had raised an objection to her acquiring another boy-friend. So who were her boy-friends? And this gymnasium she was planning – where did that fit in? And where was the money coming from? It seemed certain *she* had none and the three payments into her account, amounting to 30,000 francs, wouldn't cover a lot of work. So somewhere behind her there had to be someone who was loaded.

It might be a good idea, Pel decided, to have a word with his wife's cousin Roger, who lived in Lyons and was about the sole relative on either side of the family whom Pel could stand. Cousin Roger was an accountant and, despite his inclination to drink too much and too often, was surprisingly astute. He was also a confirmed smoker who didn't even want to give it up, so he and Pel had a lot in common.

He broached the subject over drinks before dinner. Madame Pel always liked to know what he was engaged on and even on occasion made suggestions that were helpful.

'Why would a woman as attractive as this Bronwen want to marry someone as old and silly as the Baron?' he offered as a starter.

Madame didn't waste much time on that one. 'They'd been married fourteen years,' she pointed out. 'Perhaps he wasn't quite as old and silly then.'

Since Pel was never one for seeing relatives, when he finally got around to suggesting the visit, she almost choked over her cassis. She had so many relations, Pel was convinced that laid end to end they would have stretched the length of Burgundy. And they all had money which they liked to leave to Madame when they died. Only Roger, a plump, genial man, seemed to be without any.

A telephone call brought a shriek of delight from Roger's wife. 'Be sure to bring Pel!' she yelled down the telephone. 'Roger likes him.'

Pel did the driving on the way down. As he drove he tried to explain what was worrying him.

'It's all connected somehow to this building speculation

120

that's going on,' he said, gesturing angrily. 'I'm sure of it. There are foreigners trying to acquire land in Burgundy. For building. Who are they? And what's behind it?'

'It's usually money,' Madame replied, and since she understood money, Pel was inclined to agree with her.

They had decided to avoid the motorway and stick to the country roads but near Tournus the Highways Department had dug a trench across the road and seemed prepared to defend it against all comers. The faces of both motorists and workmen suggested war was about to break out. Pel fidgeted as they waited, gesturing angrily as he argued about money. As he restarted and moved off without looking, there was a shout of '*Assassin!*' from a man climbing down from a bulldozer who had to leap for his life into the trench.

As Madame Pel had feared, the visit to Cousin Roger turned out to be very liquid and very noisy. Roger's house was full of children, all at the age when they made enough noise for the Battle of the Marne, got in everybody's way and ate enough for a zoo. There were also three dogs, six cats, four budgerigars and a tank full of tropical fish into which Roger invariably emptied the dregs of his glass.

'It makes them skittish,' he liked to explain.

After a heavy lunch and enough wine to float a battleship, Pel got Roger on one side down the garden where they both lit up and puffed away in an aura of Régie Tabac smoke as if they were in danger of being arrested for it.

'What is it this time?' Roger asked. 'Why have you come to see me? I can't imagine any man in his senses suggesting a Sunday visit to relations without a good reason when he could be dozing in front of the television. I wouldn't.'

Pel sniffed. 'I want some advice,' he admitted. 'You've heard of this case we're handling at the moment. The Baroness Raby-Labassat. There's money involved somewhere. She claimed she had some and she hired Antoine Charrieri, the architect, to draw up plans for a gymnasium.'

'You can die of heart attacks in gymnasiums,' Roger said gravely. 'I wouldn't want one. Would you?'

Pel shuddered. 'She not only had plans drawn up,' he pointed out, 'but she intended, it seems, to go ahead with it. How? As far as I can tell, she had no money of her own. So where would it be coming from?'

'Boy-friend? Somebody who thought she could make money from a gymnasium and was prepared to back her.'

'How do you make money from a gymnasium at Faux-Villecerf? The people there work all hours God sends in the fields and vineyards. They don't need a gymnasium for exercise. Their whole lives consist of exercise.'

'People from the city? From Dijon? Auxerre? Dole? Beaune?'

'Why go all that way? There are gymnasiums every-where these days. The world's gone crazy on gymnasiums. Everybody's doing exercises. Jogging —'

'Do you jog, Pel?'

'It would kill me. So who would advance money?'

'There are always people,' Roger said. 'Greedy people would advance money to anyone so long as they had a guarantee that it would double. My father used to say that thirty per cent profit was a good profit. Nowadays they expect a hundred, even two hundred. Haven't you noticed how many millionaires there are in their twenties? Once upon a time it took a man until he was fifty.'

'The money,' Pel persisted. 'Who'd supply it?'

'There's the Scoroff Finance Corporation. They'd advance anything to anybody so long as there was some-thing in it for them. There's the Société Caterin Frères. They're known to be willing to back wildcat schemes. There are plenty of those people around. There's even a new one — a Spaniard who's suddenly popped up. Name of Carmen Vlaxi.'

Pel's head jerked up. 'Would he go in for this sort of thing?'

'In my opinion he'd go in for anything. I think he's a crook.'

'I *know* he's a crook,' Pel said. 'But I didn't know *you* knew.'

11

It seemed wiser to let Madame do the driving on the way back and the following morning, Pel was still heavy-headed when he reached the Hôtel de Police. Having made his mark there, he repaired at once to the Bar Transvaal for black coffee. Back in his office he found Brochard waiting to report to him. Pel regarded him with acute distaste. He had been hoping for a quiet half hour. But Brochard was cheerfully indifferent. And it was a long story.

Brochard had spent his weekend on the shores of Lac Léman. One day, he felt, he would be truly welcomed in the Ciasca home and he looked forward to evenings of lustful dalliance on the settee while the family was out taking tourists about the lake. He had an aunt in Evian for whom he had suddenly discovered a warm and abiding affection because she had a spare room where he could stay overnight on his visits to Charlie.

When he had been introduced to the family it had finally dawned on him why she was so heavily protected. He had begun to assume their morals were stiff enough to make Martin Luther seem a lecher, but he had finally realized that Charlie was the family's pride and joy. She was the one who had been educated, the one child with some skill who had managed to get a good job. With her beauty and brains, they felt they could get her married off to someone with better prospects than an enquiry agent for an insurance company, which was what they thought Brochard was. Money and influence, they felt, might postpone the penury that was always threatening them, in a way they clearly didn't think Brochard could. The two brothers were always around to make sure she didn't put a foot wrong and compromise the scheme.

It had finally come to a head on his last visit in an argument with them all involved.

'We are responsible for our sister,' Jean-Jacques had pointed out firmly.

'An admirable attitude,' Brochard had admitted.

'And we do not trust you. You have been seeing other women.'

'Have I?' Brochard said.' I've been missing something. Where?'

'We haven't seen them but we expect to.'

Charlie snorted and gestured at Jean-Jacques with a flurry of fingers that came direct from Italy and contained not one whit of Switzerland. 'You have the imagination of a pile of sand,' she said contemptuously. 'One of these days I'll disgrace you by running off with someone from across the lake. Even perhaps a Swiss.'

Brochard hadn't let the family put him off. He'd been told by Mamma Ciasca he could call for Charlie and he was determined not to back down. The house where the family lived stood back from the road at the end of a scraggy lawn that was never cut. The front door was open and it was Italian scents – cheese and olives and ravioli and uncorked wine – that came out at you with the smell of ancient stone. The area was full of Ciascas who had followed the original bearer of the name to Switzerland. They had finally settled on the French side of the lake in a rip-roaring Italian untidiness that made the austere orderliness at the other side of the lake look like a hair shirt. A baby was crying in the next building and someone was playing a piano and singing – and holding top notes until they begged to be allowed to go free.

The Ciascas and their relations, it seemed, were as much a colony as the British and the Dutch who were bothering Pel. In spite of the influence of Swiss efficiency and cleanliness, their personality had managed to stamp itself across the whole area. It had originally been more accommodatingly French than Swiss but by this time it also had a touch of riotous Italian in the background.

As he rang the doorbell, Charlie appeared, all large eyes and spiky lashes. She grinned at him.

'You're late,' she said. 'Where've you been?'

'Busy,' Brochard said.

'Doing what?'

'Making enquiries.' Brochard played the martyr to get her sympathy. 'Things don't always go right.'

She shrugged. There were times when she was more Swiss then French or Italian and then she had an English maiden lady's rigid attitude. 'I expect it was your fault,' she said.

The simple yellow dress she wore suited her. Brochard had a feeling that there wasn't much beneath it. He also knew that apart from her the Ciasca apartment was empty.

She caught his look and grinned. 'No,' she said.

Brochard grinned back. 'It's not a bad idea,' he urged.

'I'm old-fashioned.'

'Come to that –' Brochard gestured, 'so am I. So is *that*. People have been at it for centuries.'

'No.'

'One day you'll wake up and find you're too old.'

'Not likely.'

They were still cheerfully sparring when a car drew up. From the deep baying note of the faulty exhaust, Brochard knew it was the ancient shooting brake her brothers used. A door slammed and a moment later Papa Ciasca, followed by his sons, Jean-Jacques and Gabriel, appeared. Quite unimpressed by their threats, Brochard regarded them warmly. They were all scowling and all looked alike. Papa Ciasca, thicker round the middle, was all floppy flab and looked as if he'd been stuffed by an unskilful taxidermist. The two brothers were junior versions with only slight variations between them. All were blue-jowled and black-eyed and vaguely malevolent.

'What are you doing here?' Jean-Jacques demanded.

'I came to see Charlie. What happened? Have a bad day?'

Jean-Jacques's scowl grew deeper. 'The boat broke down.'

'Always it breaks down,' Gabriel snorted.

'And you had to land your tourists?' Brochard asked.

Jean-Jacques glowered at him. It was a moment before he replied. 'Yes,' he said.

'It's that fizzy lemonade you run it on. The mixture's too rich.'

Jean-Jacques shook his head. 'One day we'll have to get ourselves a new boat.'

Mamma Ciasca appeared, in a dress on which the flowers made her eighteen stone seem more bulky than they were. She was the only one apart from Charlie who ever regarded Brochard with any warmth.

'We should give up the boat,' she said, 'and open a shop. We could sell knick-knacks and the things the Italians sell in the market at Luino.'

Jean-Jacques regarded her sullenly. 'If I open a shop,' he said, 'I'll do it in Lucerne. They say the tourists in Lucerne are stupider even than they are here.'

It was obvious one of the family rows was brewing up, noisy affairs of cataclysmic proportions that brought the neighbours out of bed.

'We'd better be going,' Charlie suggested.

'Yes,' Jean-Jacques said to Brochard. 'It's time you went.'

'I wouldn't want to outstay my welcome,' Brochard

admitted.

Ignoring the brothers, he went off happily with Charlie beside him in his car.

'That lot,' Charlie said, 'think girls should be in purdah.'

They ate a splendid meal at St-Flô and later parked the car by the lake. Breathing brandy over each other, they enjoyed a heavy session in the shadows under the trees. When Brochard took her home, he was studied with disapproval by the Ciascas but Charlie gave him a defiant kiss before tripping into the house. In the doorway she turned to wave. As she vanished, Jean-Jacques appeared by the car.

'Don't come back,' he suggested.

'Why not?'

'We have plans for Charlie.'

'Does she agree with them?'

'No. But that makes no difference.'

Brochard laughed.

'Don't come back,' Gabriel repeated over Jean-Jacques's shoulder.

'I've got the point. You don't have to beat me over the head with it.'

Papa Ciasca saw him off. 'Don't take too much notice of the boys,' he said. 'But,' he added, 'if anything happens to Charlie I'll cut your gizzard out.'

On the way to his aunt's in Evian, Brochard stopped in a bar for a last drink. As he left he almost bumped into a man who was about to enter.

'Sorry,' Brochard said.

The man ignored him and brushed past.

Outside, Brochard had come to a dead stop. He lit a cigarette and crossed the road. From a position at the other side he could see the man he'd almost bumped into leaning against the bar.

'Well, well,' he said aloud. 'Fancy that.'

*

Pel wished Brochard would shut up. His head was growing worse and they seemed to be making no progress at all.

Clos and Feray hadn't turned up, though Misset was putting on a big show of application and nose to the grindstone, and they had got nowhere with the Raby-Labassat case. And now here was Brochard droning on in a way that made Pel's head feel as though the side was about to fall off. He decided he would give Cousin Roger a miss for a while.

'That fifth man in the Boulevard Maréchal Joffre hold-up,' Brochard was saying. 'The man Nosjean and De Troq' saw in the Parc de la Columbière.'

'What about him?'

'I think I've found him. His name's Gérard Espagne.'

Pel's head lifted. 'How did you work that miracle?'

'It's a long story, *patron*.'

'It had better not be.'

Brochard grinned. 'I met this girl —'

'Which girl?'

'Her name's Carlota Ciasca.'

'You know how to make a report,' Pel snapped. 'Get on with it. Start at the beginning.'

'Yes, *patron*. She's the beginning so I'd better start with her. I got to know her. She's an illustrator. I asked her what she was doing. She said she was painting. I asked her what she was painting. She said pictures.'

'Get on,' Pel snarled.

Brochard refused to be hurried, enjoying Pel's impatience. 'I tried to arrange to see her,' he went on. 'But she said I couldn't and when I asked why, she said because she was going to see her publishers in Lyons. I said it didn't matter; I could get to Lyons all right. It's not far down the motorway. Then she said she didn't live all the time in Lyons. She only had publishers there. Often she worked from home, which was in Evian. You know Evian, *patron*?'

'Of course I know Evian. It's on the shores of Lac Léman.'

'Anyway,' Brochard continued, 'it didn't matter really. Evian wasn't much further. You just take the N6 to Macon, then the motorway to Nantua, then the main road runs alongside the Swiss border to the lake —'

Pel had heard these directions before and he sat up sharply. 'Go on,' he snapped.

'She lives at St-Flô and I went to see her. While I was there I went into a bar. I recognized this type as I came out. I nearly trod on him. He even wore the red and green windcheater Nosjean and De Troq' described. I got him at once.'

'You recognized someone from an identikit picture? Wonders will never cease.'

'I had a feeling when that picture was first issued that I knew him. But I wasn't certain. When I got back from Evian I took another look at the mug shots in the library. There he was. Gérard Espagne. Large as life and twice as nasty. Wasn't he the type who offered to set things on fire, too?'

'Yes, he was.' Pel eyed Brochard coldly. 'Well, it took long enough to get to the point,' he said, 'but perhaps it was worth it in the end. What else?'

'Well, I didn't know who he was at the time, *patron*. I just recognized a face and I wasn't certain I'd got the right guy. But I followed him home. I got his address. When I got back here I checked Records. He's got one. In Marseilles. For intimidation. That sort of thing. He also used to live here apparently, but he seems nowadays to have moved to Evian. He lives on and off with his mother. A little house on the outskirts. Rue de Genève. He was born there. Are we going to pick him up?'

'We are. But not for the robbery. And not just yet. We can't charge him with talking to Orega in the park and I've become interested in his friends.'

'Haven't we got them in custody?'

'I think he has others. Did you find out any more about him?'

130

'I didn't push it, *patron*. In case I frightened him off. I gather he's not been home for some time. But he's in Evian now. Think he's up to something down there?'

'Perhaps. On the other hand, perhaps he's just lying low. People who wish to lie low usually do it where they know the terrain and all the holes and corners. What do *you* propose to do?'

'Well, now this sheep poisoning thing's wrapped up, I thought I might keep an eye open for him.'

'How do you intend to do that?'

'Well, I'm still seeing this Charlie Ciasca. At weekends. I go to Evian.'

'Is it serious?'

'No, *patron*.'

'What is it, then?'

Brochard blushed. He blushed easily. 'I learned this Espagne goes home at weekends. So I thought when I'm down there I might keep an eye on him. Ask around. That sort of thing. See what he's up to.'

'You could do that,' Pel agreed. 'If he goes home at weekends, that's probably when he meets his friends. Find out who they are. All right. He's yours. Let's have some results. But a little faster than you make a report. And while you're there call at the Hôtel de Police there and see Inspector Bassuet. He's an old friend of mine. Ask him if anything's moving in that area.'

'Moving, *patron*? What are we interested in?'

'Building,' Pel said slowly. 'Land speculation. New housing estates for foreigners. Just ask.'

12

Since Doc Minet and Leguyader wanted no more from the body, the Baroness Bronwen Raby-Labassat de Bur was buried the following Sunday alongside the church at Faux-Villecerf. The church stood on the side of the hill and the churchyard was so steep it made Pel feel like a mountain goat.

The Indian summer they'd been having was still struggling on but a wind that had fangs and claws in it had started, and, in the shadow of the church, as it swept across the valley, it made the day feel like an arctic winter. Pel shivered in a corner as the old priest droned away at the entrance to the tomb, the carved letters, RABY-LABASSAT, catching the watery rays of a weak sun above his head. The tomb was at the back of the churchyard but, trying to avoid being seen, Pel stood by the high wall which fell away like a cliff to the road that descended to the main highway. His cold, he was convinced, had taken a turn for the worse. To depress him further, there had still been no sign of Clos or Feray. And, as far as he could make out, no Gérard Espagne. Brochard hadn't seen him again.

Not many of the village had turned out for the funeral, though Pel noticed old Sully, his eyes narrowed behind his glasses, watching carefully as if to make sure that what he was seeing was true and the Baroness really was dead and he had been reprieved. The Baron was there with Marie-

Hélène, the Baron looking a little bewildered, Marie-Hélène as though she were pleased to be shot of someone who had been a baleful influence on their lives. The Baron's three children were also there, with Gilliam and Jaunay, the Maire. In addition, there was a solitary figure in a mackintosh who turned out to be the Baroness's brother, baffled by the Catholic rites and the strangeness of the churchyard with the family mausoleums that looked like telephone boxes, the wax flowers and the photographs of the dead.

'I warned her about coming to live in France,' he told Pel in execrable French. 'But she insisted. And now look what's happened.'

About the time Pel was returning from seeing the Baroness off to her eternal rest, Brochard was entertaining Charlie Ciasca to tea in the Bar Lafitte in St-Flô. He was feeling very pleased with himself because from now on some of what it was costing him to visit her could be hidden in expenses. Pel watched expenses like a hawk but he'd told Brochard to keep his eyes open, so it would be possible to disguise a few things as bus fares, petrol and unexpected snack lunches.

Pel's friend, Inspector Bassuet, had proved a damp squib and Brochard's questions to him had brought nothing. Bassuet was a lugubrious individual — just the sort to be a friend of Pel's, Brochard thought — but he'd not heard of anything moving.

'Nothing at all,' he said. 'It's very quiet just now. I think all the villains are taking a late summer holiday. Just the usual.'

'What's that?'

'Smuggling. Swiss watches are always good sellers. They smuggle the works. But we can never get our hands on them.'

Brochard wasn't worried too much and at that moment Gérard Espagne couldn't have been further from his thoughts because he felt he could detect a distinct thawing in Charlie Ciasca's attitude.

'How about dinner tonight?' he urged. 'I know a good place on the lakeside at St-Avold.'

'You're persistent,' she said. 'Haven't you ever anything else to do?'

'Sometimes I play tennis.'

'So do I.'

'How about a game with me?'

She studied Brochard. He was tall and well built and looked as though he had a forehand which would drive her through the back of the court.

'No, thanks. I know my limitations. Playing with you would have me on my back.'

He grinned at her and she giggled. Then his grin died. So far it had been a very moral affair and Brochard was growing impatient. On the only occasions he got her away from her flat-mates the two brothers seemed to be around, and that wasn't at all what Brochard had intended. After all, she was an artist. And artists were supposed to have a bohemian life style, weren't they?

He pressed his case for dinner by the lakeside. 'You can eat on the veranda,' he said.

'I never eat on verandas,' Charlie pointed out. 'Never since I discovered that evening chills congeal the food. I can never understand why people sit on the pavement to eat. I should think all you can taste are petrol fumes. How much better it was when there weren't motor cars.'

'And the smell was of the manure from the cab horses.'

She laughed but she agreed. In the meantime, she said, she had work to do but she agreed to meet him at the bar that evening for apéritifs.

'Can't I collect you at your home?'

'My brothers will be there. And you ought to know, they like to behave like Cyrano de Bergerac.'

'I'm not going to harm you.'

'Try to convince *them* of that. They like to keep me on the

134

straight and narrow. Jean-Jacques says it's a fate worse than death.'

'There's a moon tonight. Will you still be on the straight and narrow?'

She grinned. 'I expect so. But I'll not struggle too much if *you* stray off it a bit.'

When she had gone, Brochard drove into Evian and sat with a beer in the speckled sunshine under the trees. He hadn't seen Espagne again and he suspected that, having assigned Brochard to watch him, Pel would be wanting a report before long. Finishing his beer, he drove to the Rue de Genève. Inevitably, there was no sign of Espagne, no car outside his mother's house, no Espagne happily playing ball in the garden with a little brother. It didn't take long to find he'd been around, however. The woman in the bar at the end of the street had seen him. She knew him well.

'Gérard?' she said. 'Sure, he's been here. Comes regularly. Good boy. Looks after his mother. He's been at home a lot lately.'

'Has he now?' Brochard said.

Deciding more questions might alert the man he was after, he returned to his aunt's to change his shirt, shave and clean up. As he left he bumped into Jean-Jacques. Behind him was Gabriel. They regarded him with eyes like the barrels of a shotgun.

'You're taking her to dinner,' Jean-Jacques said by way of introduction.

'That's right.'

'She's our sister.'

'Does she need a bodyguard?'

'These days she does.'

Brochard was inclined to laugh at the threat. The two brothers behaved like something out of the more purple passages of Dumas.

'Oh, ignore them,' Charlie said when she appeared. 'They behave as if I were still fourteen.'

'Are they married?'

'Both of them.'

'Haven't they enough to do looking after their wives?'

'Their wives are expected to behave.'

'So are you, it seems.'

'I've been known to slip occasionally.'

'Tonight would be a good night to slip. Let's not waste time.' The meal was a good one and they polished off a bottle of wine followed by a brandy apiece.

'I bet you're wanting to work your evil way with me,' Charlie said cheerfully.

'It's an idea,' Brochard admitted.

'I thought you might be going to suggest taking me back to your aunt's to see her etchings.'

'It crossed my mind, because she's out for the night. But I thought your brothers might be watching it.'

'You'd be right. They are.'

'So the lakeside it is.'

'I know where to go. I've been before.'

'I bet your brothers don't know about it.'

She laughed. 'My brothers know everything there is to know about the lake.'

'Because of their boat?'

'Yes.'

'I prefer sailing boats. Much more fun.'

'They don't have their boat for fun.'

'What do they have it for? Just for the tourists?'

'Officially.'

'And unofficially?'

She gave him a sidelong look and suddenly with a shock he remembered a note that had gone round the sergeants' room some time before.

*

The night was warm as they sat together on the rug from Brochard's car, staring at the lights across the other side of the lake. Brochard could feel a breeze on his cheek and it seemed to be increasing. Just below them a small area had been cleared of secondary growth among the trees and there was a huge pile of cut branches, mostly pine, lying haphazardly on top of each other. The ground around was covered with knee-deep brush, twigs and scattered fragments from the clearing.

'What's all that?' he asked.

'They open up the paths occasionally. They've just finished.'

'Nice spot.'

'Very desirable. They've been trying to get building permission here for years. The council won't allow it.'

'Why not?'

'Place of rare natural beauty. All these trees. The builders said they'd be prepared to leave them standing in clumps and put the houses in small groups among them.'

'Who were they, these builders?'

'A Paris firm. Some consortium nobody's ever heard of.'

They were clutching each other now and Charlie was just beginning to murmur 'My brothers will kill you' when Brochard stiffened and drew away.

'Well!' Charlie whispered. 'After all this time! What are you waiting for?'

'Be quiet! There's somebody down there.'

'Holy Mother of God, it must be Jean-Jacques and Gabriel! We'd better move.'

They sat up cautiously. Just below them among the trees they could see a torch. Brochard smelt petrol.

'Petrol?' he whispered. 'Here? Any boat-houses round here?'

'Nothing. That's what they're trying to get permission for. Natural thing on a lake, boat-houses. They just want to build houses to go with them.'

137

'Stay here,' Brochard said.

'What are you going to do?'

'At the moment, I don't know.'

'It's none of our business.'

'It's mine.'

Leaving the girl, Brochard descended the slope cautiously. There was a man in the undergrowth gathering twigs and laying them alongside the pile of cut branches. Brochard could now smell kerosene.

As he watched he heard the clank of a petrol can and a glugging noise. Surely to God the man wasn't scattering petrol around? But the smell was stronger now on the breeze. The man drew off a little way and Brochard saw he had a piece of rag in his hand. Laying it on the ground and picking up a can, he sloshed what smelled like kerosene on it.

'Mother of God,' Brochard breathed.

He knew exactly what the man was up to. He'd watched his father burning underbrush on the farm. The man had scattered kerosene and petrol around and was going to light it. The soaked rag was a precaution. He wasn't intending anything to explode in his face. He was going to light the rag and toss it on to the kerosene he'd scattered by the pile of branches. The petrol would attend to the rest.

The man was now standing upright, as though he were sniffing the air to get the direction of the wind. As Brochard leapt to his feet he recognized the man as Gérard Espagne and realized he had stumbled on the sort of arson that had been troubling Pel for some time.

Espagne went down with a grunt under Brochard's attack, his cigarette lighter still unused in his hand. He was winded and Brochard grabbed him by the hair and, lifting his head, banged it down on a log. Espagne went limp and Brochard was just congratulating himself on a neat arrest when he was knocked flying and found himself lying on the ground with somebody on top of him. His attacker was trying to do exactly the same to him as he'd just been doing to Espagne.

'Jean-Jacques —' He recognized the voice at once as Gabriel Ciasca's. 'It isn't Charlie who's under him. It's a man!'

The weight on Brochard was lifted, then he heard the furious voice of Charlie. Sitting up, he saw her with one of the cut branches in her hand swiping away at her brothers.

'You stupid idiots,' she said. 'Nothing's happened to me!'

Jean-Jacques was glaring at Brochard. He indicated Espagne. 'What's *he* doing here?' he asked. 'It's Gérard Espagne.'

'Do you know him?' Brochard asked.

'I see him in bars. He's a crook.'

As Jean-Jacques fished out a cigarette, Brochard knocked it from his hand. 'Light a cigarette here,' he said, 'and you're dead. The whole place's soaked with petrol. Can't you smell it, you lunatic? He was going to set the hillside alight.'

'What for? In this breeze the whole place would go up.'

'That's what he intended.'

'Name of God! We'd better let somebody know.'

'Not now you don't.'

They all swung round as a new voice joined in the conversation. Brochard had a feeling that the face of the newcomer was one he'd seen among the mug shots when he'd been looking up Espagne. It wasn't hard either to see he had a gun in his fist and that there was another man behind him.

'Who're you?'

'Never mind who I am,' the newcomer said. He gestured at Espagne who was just coming to life. 'Get him on his feet, Denot.'

The second man heaved Espagne up and started slapping his face to bring him round. The gun didn't waver.

'Who are these types?' Jean-Jacques demanded.

'No friends of mine,' Brochard assured him. 'Yours either,

139

I imagine. They'll be friends of Espagne's. And since Espagne's a crook, they'll be crooks too.'

The man with the gun grinned and Brochard knew he was right. 'But for you stupid cons,' he said to Jean-Jacques, 'I'd have nabbed one of them and been away with him before his pals arrived. I expect they were preparing things further up the slope so it'll all go up together.'

Espagne was standing on his own now without assistance and shaking his head. The man called Denot was feeling the clothes of Brochard and the Ciasca brothers. 'Knife,' he said, fishing a weapon from Jean-Jacques's pocket and tossing it into the bushes.

'What now, Lulu?' he asked.

'Get rid of them. Blow them away. We can't afford to have them around. Then we'll get to the boat and Gérard can do his stuff uninterrupted. Is he all right?'

Espagne was still rubbing his head, then, straightening up, he took a swing at Brochard. It rattled his teeth and set his brains wallowing in his head. He licked a split lip.

'Cut that out,' the man called Lulu said. 'We've not got the time for that nonsense. Get going. We'll pick you up in St-Flô and you can be across the lake and in Switzerland by morning. You'll be heading for the frontier by afternoon. Nobody will be able to connect you with this.'

Lulu's smile was thin and to Brochard it seemed almost possible to see the little wheels and cogs going round in his skull as his brain worked. He had grabbed Charlie's arm and jerked it up behind her, holding her in front of him as a shield against any attempt to attack him.

'Further up the hill,' he said to the man he called Denot. 'By that pile of cuts. We'll get rid of them there.'

'Fire your gun there,' Brochard pointed out, 'and the lot of us will probably go up. The air's full of petrol fumes.'

The thought seemed to disconcert the man with the gun and he turned to look at Espagne. As he did so, Charlie raised her knee and her spiked heel came down with all her strength on his toe. His yell of agony tore at the darkness and as he stumbled aside, he bumped into the other man. At once, Brochard aimed a blow at Espagne's stomach. As Espagne bent double, Brochard jerked his knee up and he went over backwards.

As the man with the gun straightened up, Brochard swung at him, too. It nearly broke his arm and as he turned, his fingers and wrist paralysed, he saw Jean-Jacques take a kick at the man called Denot to send him flying into the bushes. That was something about the Ciasca brothers, he thought. They knew what to do in an emergency and how to do it quickly. Thank God they were on his side for once.

As Brochard swung round, he realized he was once more alone and unarmed and the man called Lulu had grabbed the gun again. The Ciascas, all three of them, were bolting down the path towards the lake. They knew it better than Brochard did and they hadn't waited to offer help. He decided that, on his own and without a gun, discretion was the better part of valour and he set off after them, praying he wouldn't break his ankle in one of the patches of shadow.

To Brochard's surprise, he realized a light rain had started and that his face was wet. As he left the trees, he found he was stumbling through darkened streets and in and out of cobbled alleyways towards the lakeside.

He had caught up with Charlie. Concerned with their own escape, her brothers had vanished. He grabbed her hand, dragging her after him. She shrieked and almost fell as she lost her shoe. He caught her in his arms as she kicked the other shoe off, then they were running again, tripping and stumbling down a steep street to the water's edge. Behind them they could hear the clatter of feet and shouts.

'What's this place?' Brochard panted.

'Cizent.'

'Where's the police station?'

'There isn't one. It comes under St-Flô further on.'

'We'd better get along there.'

They turned down a final narrow alley and, as they burst out at the other end, they found they were near the lake. The rain was coming in a wavering mist across the water.

'Where are Jean-Jacques and Gabriel?' Charlie demanded, brushing hair from her face.

Above the sound of water beginning to gurgle in the gutters they still could hear running feet behind them.

'Wherever they are,' Brochard panted, 'they're not being followed. The bastards are all after *us*.'

And it would be important that they caught them, too. Lulu, Denot and Espagne had a lot to lose – together, Brochard supposed, with the people who were backing them. Because, he reasoned, there must be *someone* backing them. People like Lulu, Denot and Espagne didn't set fire to woods for fun and were unlikely to have the resources to make any profit out of it.

As they reached the lakeside, he saw a motor launch moored against a wooden jetty, among a cluster of hoop-topped fishing boats. A man was standing on the bow smoking a cigarette. There was no sign of anyone else because the sudden flurry of rain had driven everybody into the late bars, and they were alone.

'I bet that's their boat,' he said. 'The one they were going to use to pick up Espagne.'

'Can you handle a boat?' Charlie asked.

'No. Can you?'

'Everybody who lives on the lake can handle a boat.'

The man on the launch turned as they stepped forward, hardly visible in the shadows now that the rain clouds had hidden the moon.

'Gérard?' he whispered.

'Yes,' Brochard whispered back.

It seemed to satisfy the man on the foredeck. He turned away and bent over the bow rope. As he did so, Brochard

142

scrambled aboard and placed a foot against the seat of his trousers so that he went head-first over the side. As he fell, he grabbed at a row of fishing nets drying alongside and brought the lot down on top of him in the water in a tangle of mesh and wire and posts.

'I'll take her,' Charlie said. 'I know what to do.'

Her thin dress plastered to her body by the rain, she jumped into the wheelhouse. The whine as she pressed the starter drowned the shouts of the man struggling in the water alongside.

As the engine exploded into life, the launch began to surge against the boats moored alongside the wall. Brochard struggled to release the stern rope before they tore down the jetty and, as he did so, he caught a glimpse of a rowing boat moving away from the shore. It was about a hundred yards away, sliding across the reflection of the coloured lights outside one of the lakeside hotels. A head was silhouetted against the bright ripples, and he knew instinctively it was one of the Ciasca brothers.

He was flung to his knees as Charlie opened the throttle and the boat swung violently away from the jetty and turned to face west towards Evian. The men who had been chasing them had emerged from between the houses and were running down the jetty alongside, waiting for an opportunity to leap aboard. As he struggled to his feet, beyond them Brochard saw a figure which could only be Gabriel running for a group of parked cars. Then he was on his knees again as their port bow struck the starboard quarter of a moored launch with a crash that sent a piece of wood flying off in an erratic arc.

For a moment he thought they were going to be jammed in. He flung his weight against the rocking launch and they bounced along its side, tearing off fenders one after the other. As they drew away, a man he recognized as Espagne took a flying leap at them. He managed to reach the stern but, while he was still fighting for his balance, Brochard jabbed with the boathook and he splashed into the tumbled water behind them.

'We made it,' Brochard panted as he fell into the wheelhouse where Charlie was juggling with the wheel and the throttles.

'Not quite,' she said.

She gestured at the jetty and he saw Lulu and Denot running towards another, larger boat. As they leapt aboard and the engine roared into life, the owner emerged from one of the bars yelling with rage. As he tried to jump aboard, Denot swung a fender which hit him in the chest and sent him rolling over the side. As he vanished from sight, the boat surged away from the wall, leaving him bobbing in the water, screaming for help to the people who were now appearing on the quay.

They were roaring along the line of the shore now, bow up, the water hissing under the boat's chine, the rain blurring the windscreen in little flurries.

'I think your brothers got away,' Brochard said.

Charlie put her head out of the wheelhouse and stared astern. The other boat was well away from the wall now and heading out into the lake through a group of moored dinghies.

'They'll be all right,' she said. 'They know what to do.'

She brushed the hair from her eyes and concentrated on the wheel. The pulsating engines drowned the hiss and clatter of the water overside.

'Did it really happen?' she said in a small scared, subdued voice.

'It happened,' Brochard said grimly. 'They were going to set the hillside on fire. And it's still happening, because they have to stop us before we go the police. Perhaps we should have dived into a bar or something.'

'It'll be all right,' Charlie said. 'I know about boats.'

144

Brochard flashed her an approving glance. 'That was a bright idea,' he said. 'Stamping on his toe.'

'I hope I broke some bones.'

Brochard stared astern. Through the drizzle the hills showed black and oppressive against the sky. The lights of a car sped along the road towards Evian. 'I bet that's Gabriel,' he said.

The other boat was close on their quarter now and he could see the white of the bow wave.

'I think the bastards are catching us up,' he said.

Charlie glanced round. 'They're trying to pass us,' she said calmly. 'They'll pull in front and force us to stop. That's what the police do.'

As they reached the headland at Yvois she swung the launch round it, and the other boat followed at once. Instinctively, she swung further to port to get away and the other boat swung, too. As it drew nearer she swung away again.

'Steady on,' Brochard yelled. 'They're trying to force us ashore! We'll never get round the headland if we get any closer.'

Charlie squinted at the dashboard. 'I think they're faster than we are,' she said.

She appeared to be quite calm as she pushed the throttles as far as she could and held them there to strain the last knot from the boat. For a moment they drew away but the gap soon closed again, and for a while neither of them spoke as they listened to the banging of the boat's chine on the water.

'You're not allowed to use these speeds,' Charlie observed cheerfully. 'The lake police will be after us.'

'It's a pity they aren't,' Brochard said. 'But you can never find a cop when you want one, can you?'

For a while longer they surged along, straining their eyes towards the bow wave of the following boat. They were near the headland now and the other launch was drawing closer to the starboard side again.

'For God's sake,' Brochard said. 'Don't let them force us ashore!'

Charlie glanced over her shoulder. 'I know this lake. I've seen Jean-Jacques in action with the police. I know what to do.'

Their bow wave was slapping against the buttressed sea wall as they raced round the point. The following boat, losing ground as they turned to port, quickly caught up again and was almost alongside them again now. They could see two figures aboard and there was a flash in the darkness and a thump just behind them in the woodwork.

'They're shooting!' Brochard looked round. A car which had been keeping pace with them ashore was still with them. It seemed now to have been joined by another and he wondered if one of them was the owner of the boat Lulu had stolen, chasing his property. Then faintly above the engines he heard the siren of a police car and realized that the Evian cops hadn't been so slow after all.

They were only a few metres offshore now, close enough to hear the shouts of watchers excited by the sight of two unlit boats roaring past in the darkness. Then the second boat swung heavily to port once more.

It was bigger and faster than their own. As Charlie swung the wheel the bows of the two boats crunched together, and they bounced nearer the shore. Again the big boat swung and again the two bows crunched together.

Brochard was clinging to the dashboard to keep his balance. 'Once more,' he yelled, 'and we'll be up the beach!'

'Wait,' Charlie said. 'I am waiting.'

As the other boat came surging towards them a third time, its bow wave blue-white in the darkness, she slammed the throttles shut and flung the gears into astern. Throwing the throttles wide open again, they came to an almost abrupt halt that threw Brochard forward. The other helmsman, caught unawares, shot past their bows. Immediately, wrenching at the gear levers, Charlie flung the launch into ahead again and opened the throttles wide once more. As the other helmsman recovered himself, he found he was now on the inside with Charlie bearing swiftly down on his starboard side. Instinctively, he swung his wheel to port.

But, missing his last attempt to force them ashore, he had already swung too close himself. As the boats crunched together again, he swerved and there was a yell in the darkness. They heard the crash as the stern of the larger launch leapt clear of the water in a violent heave. A man on the deck by the wheelhouse disappeared over the side in a flurry of arms and legs, then the boat was wallowing in the surge as its own wash caught up with it. The engines screamed raggedly for a second or two, then became silent, as they heard the shriek of a police siren and saw the lights of a car swing to a stop alongside the wreck.

'They'll not trouble us again,' Charlie said with satisfaction. 'They've wiped off their propellers. They've probably even holed the boat.'

The sudden silence as she pulled back the throttles was like the easing of strained nerves, Brochard swung her towards him, feeling her small and damp in his arms as they kissed each other in delighted triumph.

'Where did you learn to handle a boat like that?' Brochard asked.

'On the lake. Jean-Jacques showed me.'

'Jean-Jacques?' He was caught by a dreadful suspicion. 'When? At night?'

'Occasionally.'

For a second Brochard gaped at her, then he turned and peered across the lake. 'Perhaps we ought to look for him,' he said.

She didn't answer and, opening the throttles a little she swung the boat towards the middle of the lake in a wide arc. The water was purple-black and for a while they circled, cut off from the world by the misty rain that shrouded the surface of the lake. Charlie put her hands on the throttles and pulled them back. They were under the shadow of the hills now, the dark water poppling against the chine.

'The boys will be all right,' she said. 'They know the lake like the back of their hands. I expect Jean-Jacques will row to Anthy. Maybe even to Nyon on the Swiss side.'

'What about the police?'

'They'll be clever if they pick up Jean-Jacques.'

'It's a long row.'

'Jean-Jacques is strong. And Gabriel will have found a car by now. They'll be all right.'

The lake was silent except for the soft murmur of the rain and the lapping of the water round the motionless boat. Ashore they could see lights grouped round the spot where they had left the wrecked launch, and more lights as late cars headed home. They heard the wavering note of a siren again.

'The police,' Brochard said. 'They'll be picking up our friends.'

Charlie switched off the engines and turned off all the lights. 'Let's just sit around for a moment and think,' she suggested.

Brochard looked warily at her. 'What are you up to?'

'It's a pity to waste such a dark night,' she said. 'I sometimes think Jean-Jacques and Gabriel are too rigid in their views. We're not likely to be interrupted here. With the rain no one can see us. And there's a cabin below and my clothes are wet. I ought to take them off.'

Brochard stared thoughtfully at her as she began to unzip her dress.

'I think,' he said slowly, 'that I ought to take you home and report to the police.'

She shrugged, struggling to peel off the wet dress. 'Someone's bound to ask questions,' she observed. 'If we arrive too soon, they'll probably pick up Jean-Jacques and Gabriel. It's all the police want: to find them out on the lake at night without a good excuse.'

Brochard studied her. He'd always respected her wishes when they'd got into clinches because of what he felt was that shining honesty all the Swiss had. It was powerful enough at times to start a guilt complex among foreigners along the lake. Now he wasn't so sure. He wasn't even certain she was as Swiss as she claimed. At the moment, she seemed more Italian than anything else — even probably pure Sicilian.

'They smuggle watches, don't they?' he said.

'Just the works. How did you guess?'

It wasn't difficult, Brochard thought. No wonder they'd never wanted him around. He wondered even if they'd found out he was a cop.

'All right,' he said reluctantly. 'We'll hang on a while.'

'But I can't stay in wet clothes, can I?'

Brochard eyed her as she kicked aside the dress and straightened up in front of him, slim and cool-looking, all the wicks turned up.

'What are we waiting for?' she said.

13

The rain had stopped and dawn was visible when they reached Evian. Charlie gave Brochard a knowing look as they stepped ashore.

'Jean-Jacques was always wrong about it being a fate worse than death,' she said. 'I told him so more than once.'

Brochard started to head for the town and she gave him a startled look. 'Where are you going?' she asked.

'I've got a job to do,' Brochard said crisply.

'Where?'

'The police station. I'm a cop.'

Her face fell. 'Name of God! Are you going to report Jean-Jacques and Gabriel?'

'No. But I've got things to report. They don't concern you or your brothers but you'd better tell them to pack it in — and fast. We're on to them. Not only us, but the cops in Evian and in Switzerland, too.'

She stared at him, her face suddenly blank. 'Thank you,' she said. 'For nothing.'

Brochard shrugged. It had been nice while it lasted but there had clearly not been much future in it.

She left him outside the police station without a word and he went inside to find the men called Lulu and Denot there already, together with the man who had been waiting on the boat. They all wore soaked clothes and were being studied by a gloomy Inspector Bassuet. Only Espagne was missing.

'I know where you can find him,' Brochard said. 'But we'd better get moving. He won't be hanging around long. But before we do that you'd better get in touch with the fire brigade. You've got a hillside near St-Avold saturated with petrol. The rain will have helped but it's still possible that if anybody tries to light a cigarette there'll be a hell of a bang.'

With the Sapeurs Pompiers alerted, Brochard climbed into the police car. They found Espagne at home but obviously already on his way. He was burning papers in the kitchen stove, watched by his mother, a wicked-looking old witch who stood with her hands in a bowl of water doing the washing up.

She gave a shriek like a factory siren as Brochard snatched up the bowl and dumped its contents in the stove. The stove gave a roar like a railway engine coming into a station and filled the kitchen with steam and black smuts, then Brochard was dragging out half-burned papers.

He had no idea what was on them but he was cop enough to guess that if Espagne was trying to burn them they were worth saving.

Caught by surprise, Espagne took a swing at him but stepped into the fist of one of the other cops who had followed Brochard inside. As he went down, Brochard swept cups and plates from the table with a crash and slapped the charred, steaming papers down and began to pat out the red from the glowing edges.

Pel was staring at his blotter. For the life of him he couldn't see anyone else guilty of the Baroness Raby-Labassat's death but the Baron. If it had been the Baron who was dead, he might have suggested one of the children or the

Baroness, because they would all have profited by his death. But the only one who could profit by the Baroness's death, as far as he could see, would be the Baron. The Baroness had become a nuisance; she was badgering him to sell his home. And, though he didn't appear particularly to want to live in it, he still regarded it as family property to be held in trust for his descendants, in particular his eldest son, Auguste.

He was still worrying it like a terrier with a rat when Brochard's telephone call arrived.

'*Patron*,' he announced. 'We've picked up Gérard Espagne.'

'Who?'

'Espagne. The last of those types who were being briefed by Orega.'

'You said "We've picked him up." Who's "we"?'

'Me and the Evian cops.'

'What for?'

'Attempted arson. That offer he made to Corvo was just a little job on the side. He didn't want to waste his talents. I happened to spot him trying to set fire to a hillside full of trees.'

'Nobody *happens* to do anything. What were you doing there? Following him?'

Brochard decided a small lie would do no harm. 'Yes, *patron*,' he said. 'I was with that girl I told you about. I was using her as a cover.'

'She'd be pleased to know that.'

'She wasn't very. He had petrol and kerosene. There were three others.'

Pel was silent for a moment or two and Brochard's voice came again, anxiously. '*Patron*, when we picked him up, he was trying to burn papers. Some of them seem to be bits of maps and some of them plans. One of them showed the area where I spotted him. It had been ringed in red. I think he was burning to a deliberate plan. It's been pretty dry lately and I bet they were thinking they could blame it all on the drought.'

'Has he talked?'

'No, *patron.*'

'Well, it's Evian's case. But I want a report. Got their names?'

'All of them. You'll be interested. Gérard Espagne; Lucien Feray; Denis Clos; Pierre-André Rougeaud — he's just a hired local boatman. They've all got form.'

'I'll come down there.'

Heading for Darcy's office, Pel found his deputy at his desk.

'Just got in,' Darcy said. 'I've been to see the Laby-Rabassat children again. They're not much to look at, *patron*, and they're also not much to talk to. Alain thinks only of his share of what his father owns. Philomène is round the bend with worry. She's even been to moneylenders. Only Auguste seems to have any pride and even that's all wrong.'

Pel explained what had happened and what Brochard had discovered. 'I'm going down there now,' he said. 'I'll get Debray to drive me. Keep an eye on things till I get back. It'll take time.'

Brochard met Pel with bandaged hands.

'It's not much, *patron*,' he said. 'I did it when I snatched the papers from the stove. The bandages are chiefly because my hands are covered with ointment. They're not as bad as they look.'

Pel nodded. Frowning. All the way down he had been remembering the scrap of paper Darcy had found at the Chateau de Faux-Villecerf. *N74 to N6. N6 to Macon. Motorway to Bourg and then to Nantua. Road runs alongside Swiss border to lake.* It seemed to indicate as clear as daylight that Bronwen Raby-Labassat had been to Evian, and he wondered why. Surely Espagne and Feray and Clos weren't included among her boy-friends, too!

Brochard spread the remains of the maps he had rescued on Bassuet's desk and they bent over them. They appeared to be blown-up copies of Michelin maps tinted with water-colour to indicate land levels. On several of them buildings were indicated but major names had been painted out. With them were scraps of plans, half-burned and indicating very little.

'Well, that one seems to indicate St-Avold,' Bassuet said. 'Right where the uproar last night occurred. The shapes and levels are right. They'd obviously got hopes of building there and they've got the right type of house. Look at the comment: "Split levels". Just the thing for steep slopes. And this — "Tennis court. Restaurant. Bar."'

Bassuet and Brochard had been working hard and had identified most of the areas on the copied maps and produced the appropriate Michelin guides. The plans indicated nothing.

Pel gestured at one of the maps which seemed to show land near Sémur. 'This one could fit in here,' he stabbed a finger, '– but there's no name, so we're guessing. This one –' He pulled forward another of the charred sheets, '– this could be here again. In the Evian area. This blue surely represents water. But they haven't shown the contours on this one so it might apply to somewhere in the Camargue or the Vendée for all we can tell.'

He peered at the minute writing in the margin. 'Complex of apartments and dwelling-houses,' it said, then the rest was burned away. Later came the words 'Restaurant and swimming pool'.

'We'd better check up,' he said. 'Where might it be, do you think?'

'St-Jean de Mont? Sète?' Bassuet shrugged. 'There's no indication of location. Which seems to indicate someone was acting a bit shiftily.'

He brought in the prisoners one by one for questioning. None of them was talking, which made Pel more than ever certain that someone with muscle was involved. If not Vlaxi, then some new villain up from Marseilles where they seemed to breed like rabbits.

He listened to the questions and interposed a few of his own. But they got nowhere and there was little they could do about it because the case belonged to Evian, though Bassuet promised to send on all reports and depositions and keep Pel well in touch. They had to be satisfied with that.

As they left, Brochard drew Pel on one side. 'It's all right, *patron*,' he said quietly. 'I had extra copies and colour photographs made of every one of those papers I found. And, as the arresting officer, I'm keeping them.'

For Darcy, sitting in Pel's chair, it had been a long day. There had been another hold-up, this time in the Rue de la Victoire, and a stabbing in the Rue de Rouen area. They had both needed Darcy on the spot because no one had been arrested or even seen. Fortunately, the hold-up merchant had been as dim as Jean-Pierre Orega, and the knife which had carved up a young prostitute carried fingerprints already known to the police.

Though they'd been easy, they'd been time-consuming and, with all the other things that had cropped up, had made it a long day. Darcy closed the files on the desk with some satisfaction. He was just heading for the door when the telephone rang. He took the call standing up.

'This is Raby-Labassat,' it said. 'Honoré Raby-Labassat. Can I come and see you?'

'Why not see the boss, Chief Inspector Pel?'

'Very well, tomorrow?'

'Why not now? If it's important, he'll come out to see you when he gets back. Of if you prefer it, I'll come myself.'

The voice sounded agitated and uncertain suddenly. 'No. It's probably not that important. I think I'll come down in the morning.'

As the telephone clicked the experienced Darcy stared at it, frowning. There was something in the wind, he decided. It seemed, in fact, as if it might be a good idea to drive out to Faux-Villecerf there and then and discover what it was.

Pel and Brochard arrived back late and only Claudie Darel was still around. Brochard's hands were beginning to be painful by this time and he looked tired because he had had no sleep the night before. He was about to start sorting out the papers they had brought back when Pel pushed him gently aside.

'Leave them,' he said. 'Put them on my desk and go home. We'll get Lagé to look into where they might fit. He can check all applications that have been put in or granted, even plans that have simply been discussed. The planning office usually knows what might be coming up. You can help later. It'll give your hands time to heal.'

As Brochard began to head for the stairs, Pel sat in his chair and lit a cigarette. Just a last one, he thought, so he could then chew a fresh breath capsule and arrive in front of his wife smelling of roses instead of like an old exhaust pipe.

He was beginning to unwind a little when the internal telephone went. It was Claudie. 'I thought you'd gone, *patron*', she said. 'Aimedieu rang. He's at Faux-Villecerf. With Inspector Darcy. There's been another one.'

'Another one what?'

'Death. I'm just organizing Doc Cham and Doc Minet. I've informed Forensic and all the others.'

'Who is it?'

'The Baron, *patron*. He's been found in the cellar.'

14

Auguste Raby-Labassat was already at the chateau. With him, sitting in a chair in the huge kitchen, her face blank as if she were shocked, was Marie-Hélène. Darcy was prowling about the room.

'It's hit her hard,' Auguste said. 'They'd just moved into the house from the cottage. I think my father fancied the house really. He just couldn't stand being in the same place as Bronwen. He seems to have gone down to the cellar to fetch wine for tomorrow. Marie-Hélène says he was intending to celebrate with a little party for me and my wife. She persuaded him we should drink something a little better than his own wine.' Auguste sighed. 'It wasn't really very good.'

'Who found him?'

'Marie-Hélène,' Darcy said. 'She'd been to the cottage. She couldn't find him when she returned and eventually she found him at the bottom of the steps. There were two broken bottles.'

'It must have happened soon after he telephoned me,' he went on. 'I came straight out. Whoever did it probably even heard him talking to me, saw Marie-Hélène leave, and followed him to the cellar.'

The cellar was a big place with stone-flagged floors and an arched ceiling, and a surprising number of bottles for a family that was supposed to be poor. But then Pel glanced at the labels and saw that most of them were the Baron's own wine and that none of the rest was of particularly good quality.

The body lay at the bottom of the stone steps that led down from the kitchen and a chalk line had already been drawn round it. About it was spilled wine, shattered glass and the necks of two bottles, both still corked. The police photographer was busy with his camera, photographing the body from every possible angle.

'Did he fall?' Pel murmured. 'Or was he pushed?'

Doc Minet looked up. 'If he fell,' he said, 'as he appears to have done, he must have come down those steps at a hell of a speed. Which seems to indicate he might well have been pushed. He appears to have hit his head on the stone pillar there at the bottom.'

Doc Cham looked up from his position beside the older man. 'Except,' he said, 'that's not what happened.'

There was obviously more to come. 'Go on,' Pel said.

'There's blood on the pillar there,' Cham pointed out. 'But no sign of hair or tissue. The back of his head's knocked in. But not, I suspect, by collision with a stone pillar. It looks to me as if he was hit by a heavy blunt instrument, the natural successor to the club, man's first tool of aggression and the most common of murder weapons.'

'The blood on the pillar's only a smear,' Minet pointed out. 'It could have been placed there. Deliberately. It's rough stone but there's no hair or tissue adhering to it.'

'What about the blood on the floor?'

Leguyader appeared from the shadows in the back of the cellar. He was obviously in top gear, at full throttle and with all stops open. He was at his pompous best and, judging by the way he looked at Cham, the honeymoon between them had come to an end.

'A great deal can be gleaned from the shape of blood spots and splashes,' he said. 'The great criminologist, Alexandre Lacassagne, noted the relationship between the

158

shape of blood spots and the position of the victim.'

'Facts,' Pel snapped.

'These are facts,' Leguyader snarled back. 'As we've discovered on many occasions, drops of blood falling from a moving object hit a flat surface obliquely and leave a spot shaped like an exclamation mark. Two ovoid shapes with pointed ends, the points directed to each other, one long, one small. The point of the smaller spot indicates the direction of travel. There are spots by the door at the top of the stairs and spots down here. The ones we see here indicate he fell down the stairs all right but not necessarily from the top.' Leguyader paused. It was obvious the three of them had been having an argument and Leguyader had prevailed. 'But that's not all. We have another interesting thing. He seems to have been carrying two bottles. *Seems*, I say. They appear to be a cheap Chablis, which I gather was one of the favourites of the Gaussac woman. He was obviously intending they should celebrate their return to the chateau.'

'We know that,' Pel snapped.

Leguyader wasn't put off in the slightest. 'This is the point —' Pel waited impatiently. Leguyader would inevitably go on to the very end. But, knowing that whatever else he was, he was an expert, Pel held on to his temper.

'When you carry two bottles of wine,' Leguyader continued,' you usually carry them both in the right hand with the necks between the fingers, leaving the left hand free to close doors, switch off lights, et cetera.'

'If you're right-handed.'

'He was,' Leguyader said smugly. 'I took the trouble to find out. In which case, the fingerprints of the right hand should be on the necks of the bottles which, you'll notice, remain unbroken. Prélat's examined them and he tells me there are none. He thinks they've been wiped. Why? People fetching wine from the cellar wipe the bottles in the kitchen, not in the cellar. And, in any case, there's no cloth down here. Take a look around you. So — if he *did* wipe them before taking them upstairs, where did the cloth go? Not with him. Because he didn't make it back to the kitchen.'

Trust Leguyader's sharp eyes to spot the irregularity, Pel thought.

'This brings us to another thing,' Leguyader went on. 'If he simply stumbled on the stairs, the bottles would surely have been dropped *there* in his efforts to regain his balance. That seems unlikely, though, because they're here near the body on the floor of the cellar. If he'd released them on the stairs, in fact, one of them might perhaps not have been broken. It might even have rolled undamaged to the bottom. As it is, both broke. And broke here in the cellar. Moreover,' Leguyader paused, 'if they'd come from up there on the stairs, the wine would have shot with the splinters of glass across the stone floor in a rough line from the stairs into the cellar. Wine's like any other liquid. You'd have roughly the same affect you have with blood, but on a larger scale. Instead, you'll notice it's made a circular splash pattern. And the patterns are virtually alongside and one on each side of the body. It think they were taken from the rack *after* he died and were dropped and broken to indicate exactly what we were expected to believe.

Leguyader smiled. 'I think,' he ended cheerfully, 'that he fell going *down* the stairs, not going up. And I don't think he was carrying any wine.'

Doc Minet confirmed the theory. 'Something hard and heavy,' he said. 'Two blows, we think.'

'There should be a heavy hammer down here,' Leguyader said. 'I've talked to the son. It was used when the family brewed their own beer. To bang the taps into the barrels. It hasn't been used for years for that but it was kept to prop open the door, which had a habit of swinging to. It should be at the top of the stairs. But it's not. It's missing.'

It sounded a good and careful deduction commensurate with the facts.

Returning upstairs, Pel found Darcy talking to Aimedieu. 'Who else was in the house?' he asked.

'Nobody. Just the Baron. Marie-Hélène had just left. But that doesn't mean a thing. The door's always open. In this village, nobody locks doors except at night. Anybody could have walked in, and most of the village know their way around because a lot of them had worked at one time or another in the house or the garden. Marie-Hélène says he *might* have fallen. We know he liked a drink. Sometimes one too many.'

'How long was she at the cottage?'

'She says half an hour.'

'I'd better talk to her.'

Marie-Hélène was still sitting in the kitchen. She was ashen and looked broken. 'He'd been drinking,' she admitted. 'Something was worrying him.'

'Do you know what?'

'This place, I think. It's evil. It's affected everybody. He liked it as it was and Bronwen was always wanting him to spend money on it that he didn't possess.'

'You *know* he didn't.'

'I knew everything about him.' There was a touch of pride in the old woman's voice. 'I always did. Ever since I was a young girl. He was a good man. He always stood up for the village. Years ago he stood up against the Conseil Général over the building of a new road. It would have made things easier because it's always hard to get big tractors and trailers through, and when they're loading outside the bakery, you can't get past and have to reverse and go round by the church. But that's how it's been for generations and people who live here don't think in terms of what's easy but how it's always been.'

She sighed. 'There was talk once of re-routing the river in the valley and doing away with the bridge there, but he stood up against that, too. There was even a plan drawn up in 1975 that included an artificially made beach and a restaurant and bar, so that people could sailboard. There was a village meeting. We thought it would bring people from as far away as Dijon on hot afternoons and we didn't want that.'

'Couldn't the Baron have profited by it?'

'Yes. Someone — I think it was the Maire — tried to persuade him and said there was money in it. But he wouldn't hear of it. He was an honest man. A bit silly and more easily persuaded nowadays, because he was old, but he was right. This is rural France and we don't want to be the playground for people from the cities.'

'Was anybody else involved in this project besides the Maire?'

'The Englishman. Gilliam. I think he was for a while. But nothing came of it. They couldn't get enough support. Perhaps if they had, something would have happened and they would have overridden the villagers.'

'That wouldn't have made Jaunay a very popular maire.'

'He wouldn't have worried. He has money. He'd just have moved away.'

It was not until late the next day that they found out about the hammer. It was in the cottage. Marie-Hélène was making pressed beef in a tin with a plate on top and the hammer was being used as a weight.

'I reckon he was killed with his own mallet,' Darcy said. 'I've found his tool box. He'd been repairing a cupboard door in that room his mother used. His tools were there and the cupboard door's off. He's been chiselling away at the wood. There are chips on the floor. But the wood's oak and you can't chisel oak without a mallet. Apparently, the one he uses is an old-fashioned type with inset lead strips on the head. I think he had it in his hand and when whoever killed him appeared, he came down the stairs to meet them. He was still carrying the mallet and he put it down to talk. As he turned away, it was picked up and used to hit him. I think the first blow sent him staggering down the steps and it required another — in the cellar — to kill him.'

Auguste Raby-Labassat seemed already to be making plans to move into the chateau.

'My children will enjoy living here,' he said. 'Particularly in the summer.'

'What about the winter?' Pel asked.

'We'll do as my father did and live in the great kitchen.'

'You care a lot about this place?'

Auguste turned. 'Of course I care,' he said. 'But I'm not sentimental. Sentimentality's a failure of feeling. But if I live here, it will help keep this corner of France as the French want it. Any government worth its salt would prevent the invasion of France by foreigners.'

'Are you concerned about that, too?'

'Very much so.'

'We're supposed to belong to a common Europe. We're not foreigners any more. Nobody is. We're Europeans.' Pel didn't believe for a minute he was anything but a Burgundian but he was anxious to see how Auguste regarded it.

Auguste's views were clear. 'I can't afford to be broad-minded,' he said. 'To me, this is *France*.'

'Would you go to any lengths to keep it so?'

Auguste regarded him sternly. 'Any lengths,' he said.

Alain Raby-Labassat's attitude when he arrived was very different. 'We should sell,' he said at once. 'We're all in debt — except perhaps Auguste.'

He had appeared with his sister, and ever since they had been huddled in a corner of the chilly salon earmarking items for their future possession.

'Under the law,' he said,' we're entitled to a third share of the estate. That's the law. And his estate includes all this junk.'

'This junk,' Pel pointed out, 'is antique. It could be very valuable.'

'All the more reason why we should sell it and split the proceeds.'

'The place would look very odd if the rooms were emptied.'

'That's not my affair.'

'Do you know of a will that could alter things?'

'He never left a will,' Philomène said, and Pel noticed that both of them kept referring to their father as if he were a complete stranger. 'He was gaga. I know this: He wouldn't have left *me* much. He thought I was a fool. Come to think of it, I do, too, now. But that's by the way. Still, he was nobody to talk, was he? That damned Bronwen was nothing to write home about. I wish I knew how much there was. If we shared it out we'd all be better off.'

'Except, perhaps, Auguste, who's proposing to live here.'

They spoke almost together. 'That prig,' they said.

Pel decided he didn't like them very much.

At the time of his father's death, Alain had been playing the clarinet at St-Eloi and the other members of his group were prepared to vouch for him. Philomène had been at home with three teenage children to prove it, watching a 007 film on television. Auguste claimed he had been at his office working and his wife agreed he had been late home. He had even been seen leaving his office by a woman with an apartment across the road. But Aimedieu had been to check the place and had noticed there was a back door, so he could have left by it and returned the same way to depart finally by the front door where he could be seen by the woman across the road. They would all benefit in a small way by their father's death, though it seemed there would hardly be enough to make murder worthwhile.

'There's very little money,' Auguste insisted. 'I'm sure of that. And some of the contents will have to be sold. I'll just keep the most valuable articles and get rid of the poor stuff.'

'Your brother and sister seem to want you to sell the lot.'

'I've thought of that.' Auguste's smile was crafty. 'I'll appeal to the Ministry of Fine Arts and National Treasures. They'll back me, I'm sure. I'd like to make an inventory for them.'

'When?'

'Now. Before Alain and Philomène get their hands on anything.There are folios of drawings done by my great-grandfather for a start. They're valuable, I feel sure, not only artistically but historically. Will that be possible? I'm quite happy to have a policeman around while I do it.'

There was another one in the village whom it might be a good idea to see while they were about it. Two, in fact: Jaunay and old Sully.

Jaunay was out on one of his sites but old Sully was sitting in his shabby little living-room. They knew he was there although the shutters were closed against the sun. He met them at the door, dancing with excitement. 'It wasn't me,' he said at once. 'It wasn't me. 'I didn't kill him. I never touched him.'

'Who?'

'The Baron. The Baron, of course. Him.'

'How did you know the Baron was dead?'

'It's all over the village. Everybody knows. Everybody. Madame Laniel next door told me.'

'How did she learn?'

'From Madame Croix, I expect. That's where she always gets her news. Madame Croix. She's a widow and she keeps her ears open. Madame Croix. It was the man in the car did it. He was the one. The man in the car.'

Pel remembered the poacher, Arnaud, had mentioned seeing a car in the village about the time the Baroness had disappeared.

'What was this car like?'

'Black.'

'What sort?'

Sully didn't know. He'd never had much to do with cars, he said. 'Perhaps a Renault. But it might have been a Peugeot. I can't say.'

'But you saw it in the village?'

'Yes. It's been hanging about for a day or two.'

'Is it still here?'

'No, no, no. It's gone. Gone.'

'Did you see who was driving it?'

'No. A man, I suppose. But it might have been a woman. Women drive cars. But I think it was a man. Or maybe a woman. I don't know.'

'Did you see its number?'

'Yes. Well, no. That is, some of it. It had a 2 in it. But I don't know. I'm not good on numbers. Or cars. I never owned one. Never.'

It didn't sound like Jaunay's car, which was a yellow Peugeot and it didn't sound like Auguste Raby-Labassat's. He drove a silver-grey Citroën BX15. Alain, they knew, had an elderly Peugeot, coloured fawn, and the best Philomène could manage was the ancient Deux Chevaux painted psychodelic pink with flowers.

'How about Gilliam?' Pel asked.

'Red,' Darcy said. 'Orange-red. I saw it outside his house. His wife has one the same colour. You remember we saw her driving off in it.'

'Could red seem to be black in a bad light?'

'It could.'

Sully's neighbour, Madame Laniel, was no wiser than Sully. She was a thin vinegar-faced creature but she seemed to have sharp eyes and she remembered a car hanging around the village. 'Would it be the type who wanted to buy my house?' she asked.

'Which type?'

'He said he was a builder.'

'Jaunay?'

'No, it wasn't him. Perhaps he was an architect.'

'Name of Charrieri?'

'No. He said he was working for a group who were buying up property. They wanted my house.'

'Were you prepared to sell?'

'No. I've lived here ever since I was married. He said he wanted to make a hairdressing salon out of it.'

'A hairdressing salon? Here? In Faux-Villecerf?'

'That's what he said. We could certainly do with one.'

'What was he like?'

'Little. Fair-haired.'

'What about this car?'

'It was a small car. Like Monsieur Vardie's.'

'And the driver?'

'I couldn't see him. It was getting dark when I saw it.'

'What about the number?'

'There was an X in it. And I saw some of the number. A 2 and a 3 and a 5. I didn't look very carefully but I noticed that. It went past too quickly to catch anything else.'

Monsieur Vardie turned out to be the baker and an enquiry at the bakery elicited the information that his car was a Renault 304, dark green.

'Which,' Darcy said, 'could look black at dusk.'

15

Pel sat at his desk, scowling at the reports in front of him. He was dying for a cigarette but felt he hadn't allowed enough time to elapse since the last one.

Knowing what was going through his mind, Darcy edged his own packet across the desk, moving it closer as if it were moving of its own accord. In the end, Pel could resist no longer. Looking the other way, he reached out and took a cigarette as if he had done it without thinking. Darcy grinned and reached across the desk with his lighter.

Dragging the smoke down until it looked as though it might come out through the lace-holes of his shoes, Pel coughed as if he were dying of consumption and began to feel better.

As they talked, Claudie Darel appeared to announce that Pel was wanted in the Chief's office.

The Chief met him with a smile. 'Brochard did well,' he said, producing the brandy bottle and obviously in a good mood. 'Is he still down there in Evian?'

'He's gone back,' Pel said. 'To tie things up. After all, he was the one who sorted it out. But, it always takes longer to handle the paperwork than make an arrest. Most of the time we're neck-deep in it. But Evian's pleased. They were in danger of losing about fifty hectares of forest overlooking the lake. The maps Brochard found seemed to indicate somebody's anxious to build there.'

'Any idea who?'

'Seems to be a firm called Branco. We'll check them.'

'What about the plans? Anything been submitted?'

'No. And some of them seem to concern places other than round Evian. We're trying to decide where.'

Later in the day, Darcy's theory about the Baron's mallet was proved to be correct. It was found on the Aignay rubbish tip. It had been dropped into the communal garbage bin at Faux-Villecerf, an enormous grey and green plastic affair on wheels which was hoisted up and tipped by hydraulic power supplied by the refuse cart. 'Very clean, very efficient,' the foreman in charge said. 'No flies. No smells. Well, not many. Not in winter, anyway.'

It had been found by the man emptying the cart, who had decided it was just what he was wanting for use at home. He had helped himself to it and was reluctant to give it up. It revealed nothing except traces of blood on the head which matched the Baron's. It had been well wiped and there were no fingerprints.

'People know what to do these days,' Pel said gloomily. 'They get their tips twice nightly from television who-dunits. There's something about all this that smells less of inheritance than of speculation.'

'Would people murder for *that*?' Darcy asked.

'They seem to be prepared to set places on fire. We have four people in custody. Then there are those two hundred bags of cement Jaunay ordered. That's a lot of cement to reorganize a stables into a gymnasium. Could Jaunay have been accepting bribes? Suppose Gilliam offered more than that three thousand francs to Bronwen. Suppose he was in deeper than he said. Suppose things had gone wrong and he stood to lose a lot of money. He has a temper. That we know because we saw his wife with a black eye.'

*

169

When they talked to Jaunay he looked uncomfortable.

'Well, there *was* a plan,' he admitted.

'And it fell through,' Pel said. 'Why?'

'I don't know.'

'Were any sweeteners offered? There must have been people who were willing to push this thing through.'

'I suppose there were.'

'They accepted bribes?'

'I expect so.'

'Who were they?'

'I don't know. The Baroness didn't tell me anything.'

'Could it have been you who offered them?'

Jaunay looked alarmed. 'I haven't got that sort of money.'

'But you were prepared to take advantage of them?'

'I'm a builder. I need to build — and the bigger the project and the longer it lasts, the better it is for me and my people.'

It seemed a good idea to look once more at the papers Brochard had rescued from the Espagne kitchen stove. Some of them clearly didn't concern Evian but someone was obviously eager to do some building. It seemed important to identify the locations.

They took over the lecture room at the Hôtel de Police and spread the papers on tables to study them. In addition, there was a large map of Burgundy and its neighbouring areas and the appropriate Michelin maps. Claudie, who'd been watching everything, was running the show.

They started with a check on all the places where recent developments had been suggested. Concentrating on country areas, they found there were more than they had expected.

'There are agencies all over England,' Claudie said. 'They deal in anything from chateaux to small businesses. They're even building high-rise apartment blocks and giving them English names like "Oxford" and "Pall Mall". They're everywhere. Le Touquet. Boulogne. La Baule. Brittany. Anywhere there's a bit of water.'

'*They*'re surely for the rich,' the Chief said.

'No,' Claudie insisted. 'There's something for everybody. It's an invasion as big as D-Day. Northern France welcomes them. They've been going through a bad patch up there so anything that brings employment is welcomed. When someone applies to buy land for planning the first question they're asked is "How many local people will be employed?" If it's more than five they get permission straight away.'

'I think we have to find who's interested in these places marked on Brochard's map,' the Chief said. 'Council records will show if there have been applications.'

'I think we'd do better to check places where land's been destroyed,' Pel advised. 'And find who built on *them*.' He gestured at Brochard's sheets. 'There are plenty to go on. There's one here for a complete holiday village. A hotel with split-level dwellings and apartments. *And water*. That's surely water indicated in blue.'

As Pel returned to his office Lagé appeared. Slow as he was, he was very thorough and when he got his teeth into something he never let go. He'd been taken off his fraud enquiry and had been examining records from the level of local mairies up to the level of the Conseil Général to find where the holiday village was planned.

'*Patron*,' he said, 'that blue on the drawing Brochard found: it *has* to be a lake or something. And these split-level buildings seemed to indicate lakes with steep sides. But France's full of lakes. There's the Lac de Serre-Ponçon, the Lac d'Allos, the Lac de la Forêt d'Orient, the Lac de St-Cassien, the Lac de Ste-Croix, the Lac des Carces —'

'Never mind how many,' Pel said irritably. 'What about lakes in this area?'

'There's really only the Lac de la Liez and the Reservoir de la Mouche near Langres. South, there are more. Near

Pontarlier there's the Lac de St-Point and the Lac de Joux. Near Annécy there's the Lac d'Annécy, and there are one or two south of Bourg-en-Bresse, together with a whole lot of smaller ones further west. All big enough to make a pleasant outlook for someone wanting to develop an estate on the shore. But nothing round here.'

Pel said nothing and Lagé went on. 'I've also been checking all the areas where woods were burned down. I came across five more dubious ones. Planning permission was applied for in three cases. For development. One was granted because it's now five years since the fire. In the case of one that was *not* granted, the speculators – a Paris outfit – said they'd apply again. The other three – all recent – have *not* been applied for, but I was told applications might well arrive eventually. Rumours have been floating about. Judging by what I could find out, the application that *was* granted, at Larin-et-Musset, and the one that wasn't, at Mont Gathier, both came from the same source, but the names of the companies – Financements Générals Bourgignons and Commandites de Dijon – were different. Both are Anglo-French.'

16

It seemed to be time to contact Superintendent Goschen at Scotland Yard again.

Pel lit a cigarette and did a lot of throat clearing. Then he asked Claudie for coffee and, to give himself courage before he picked up the telephone, had a brandy with it. In the end it turned out to be easier than he had expected. He and Goschen seemed to be developing a rapport that was of advantage to both of them.

'We've checked on all places recently developed by speculators,' Pel pointed out. 'We found the builders were honest; though, of course, they were all expecting large profits. But the money behind them seems to be coming from Anglo-French consortiums who're developing properties in France. Have you anybody that fits?'

'There's our friend, the Dutchman I mentioned,' Goschen said. 'Cornelius. We've found he's in contact with a man over here.'

'Your English speculator?'

'Welsh, actually. Name of David Lloyd Jones. And there's another − a Frenchman.'

'Got any names?'

'No. None.'

'What about Carmen Vlaxi? Does he ring a bell?'

'Not with this one. This seems to be a small group.'

Pel sat back, scowling. They had absolutely no proof, but

Carmen Vlaxi was the only man he could think of. Despite the mutual bloody-mindedness of 'interview and questioning', Orega still hadn't talked. He had finally admitted that the security van had been part of the hold-up but insisted the idea was his and his alone. Still nobody believed him. But though his raid had achieved nothing, it had brought up the name of the fifth man, Gérard, and it was he who had provided a link with Vlaxi.

Vlaxi's headquarters were in Paris and Pel hated Paris. Though to others it was known as the City of Light, the City of Kings and Emperors, to Pel it was just crowded.

Contacting the Quai des Orfèvres, the Paris police headquarters, he learned that Vlaxi was, in fact, spending a weekend at his country estate at St-Symphorien-le-Grand near by.

'Manoir de Ste-Euphrasie,' Darcy said immediately. 'I looked it up a long time ago.'

'In the yellow pages?' Pal asked sarcastically. 'Under "Gangster"? I think we ought to pay him a call.'

The house was big, not big enough to be called a chateau but roomy and very rustic, surrounded by gardens and trees and not overlooked, Pel noticed, from any direction. It was ideal for a man of Vlaxi's interests and habits.

Vlaxi himself was a small man with large horn-rimmed spectacles and an innocent intellectual expression. He looked, in fact, like a professor of physics. He was a handsome little devil, too, with a fine nose, grey eyes and brown hair immaculately cut, and the figure of a torero. His clothes made Pel feel like a third-rate plumber called in to attend to the drains. He was surrounded by a group of men he claimed were his advisers and accountants, there for a business meeting, but they all looked remarkably like

174

bouncers from a night club. There was also a girl. There was *always* a girl. Like all the others, this one looked as though she had strayed off a film set. Where, Pel wondered, did they find them? And why did girls of such breathtaking beauty, who could have picked up a financier without changing gear, go for a man with a background like Vlaxi's?

'Chief Inspector Pel,' Vlaxi said, holding out his hand. 'We've never met but I've heard of you.'

Pel ignored the proffered hand. It didn't seem to perturb Vlaxi. 'What can I do for you?' he asked.

'Probably nothing,' Pel said coldly. 'I'm interested in a Baroness Raby-Labassat.'

'The woman who was found at Vieilles Etuves. Of course. I read about it in the paper.'

'Did you know her?'

Vlaxi laughed. 'Me? I'm just a minor figure engaged in finance. Why would I know a baroness?'

'You might be interested in this one. She needed money, and she claimed to have found some. Did she come to you?'

Vlaxi spread his hands. 'Why should she come to me? I'd never heard of her until I read of her in *Le Bien Public.*'

'Your name's been mentioned.'

'Who by?'

By Cousin Roger, to be exact, Pel thought. But he could hardly say so. Cousin Roger's view wasn't evidence and mentioning his name might well get him rubbed out. He gestured. 'The name cropped up.'

Vlaxi shrugged. 'What was she wanting money for? I'm not against going into things if they're profitable but I'm not in the market to make small loans. I leave that to the banks.'

'It was to construct a gymnasium from a stable block.'

Vlaxi laughed again. 'I play golf,' he said. 'At St-Emilien. I don't see myself leaping round a gymnasium dressed in tights. Was it a big gymnasium?'

'Big enough. What do you put your money into?'

'Things that make profits.'

'Ever gone in for building projects?'

Vlaxi was still smiling. 'They take too long to mature.'

'Not all of them.'

The smile didn't slip. 'You mean there's money to be made that I don't know about?'

They were only fencing and Vlaxi was good at it.

Pel glanced about him. 'Nice place you have here. Cost a lot, did it?'

Vlaxi smiled. 'My places always cost a lot. They have to be big. I have a lot of staff.' Hired gunmen, Pel decided. Bodyguards. Shifty accountants who could fiddle balance sheets. Crooked lawyers who could find ways round the law.

'What are you into?'

'Into?'

'What are you running? Why are you here? What are you doing?'

'I bought some vineyards round here. A chain of supermarkets. A group of garages.'

Maurice Tagliatti's old properties, without a doubt, Pel decided. He even had a feeling that he'd seen one of the men standing behind Vlaxi once standing behind Tagliatti.

'Is that why you came to see me?' Vlaxi asked. 'To enquire what my business is here?'

'No,' Pel said. 'Just to make your acquaintance. I'm always interested in newcomers to the district.'

Vlaxi beamed. 'Then I'm delighted to meet you, Chief Inspector. Can I offer you anything? A drink, perhaps?'

A girl? A motor car? A bribe?

'No, thanks,' Pel said. 'In fact, I'll be off. I was just passing and thought I'd call.'

It was a warm day so they stopped at the bar in the village for a beer.

The bar was set back from the road and was fronted by a

176

dusty car-park where a group of old men were tossing boules. They were watched by an old woman, two small girls and a dog. There was a whiff of cooking hanging in the air, then someone lit a Gauloise. To Pel it smelled like Heaven and he drew it in as though it were the breath of life.

Darcy broke in on his thoughts. 'Not much there, *patron*,' he said, gesturing towards the house they had just left.

'I didn't expect to find much,' Pel admitted. 'I just wanted to meet him, to know what he looked like. You can bet your last franc that from now on when anything unlawful happens around here he'll be involved in it.'

They didn't seem to have picked anything up but when they arrived back at the Hôtel de Police, Claudie Darel followed them into Pel's office.

'That farm at Tar-le-Petit. *patron*,' she said. 'The one the Chief mentioned. The one where the farmer died and it was left vacant and ended up vandalized. I've just heard another planning application's been put in. I thought you'd like to know.'

'What's it for this time?'

'First they put in for a night club and bar but they've changed it to a motel because it's close to the N6. Large-scale thing. Swimming pool. Two restaurants. They claim it's just what the area needs.'

'Where did you get this?'

'At the offices of the Conseil Général at the Palais des Ducs, *patron*. It was spotted at the Préfecture. It seems to have got past the Mairie at Tar and the office of the Sous-Préfecture without comment.'

'I bet somebody's palms were greased. Who put it in?'

'Firm called Paillat, Hégrion and Michel, of Lyons. I've talked to them. They say they were instructed by a finance firm called Capitalisation Français. *They* claim they're interested only because the land's there and available and they could make money by financing a project such as this.'

'Who *are* Capitalisation Français?'

'Paris firm. Dozens of stockholders. I got hold of a list. No names we know.'

'I bet there are a few we'd like to know. Whose is the actual name on the application?'

'An architect from Lyons.'

'Not Charrieri?'

'Definitely not Charrieri, *patron*. It's another Michel. Georges-Charles Michel. He's brother to Michel, the lawyer at Paillat, Hégrion and Michel.'

'Very interesting.'

'There's also a Gilbert Tussot involved. He's an accountant at St-Frond. He once did work for Maurice Tagliatti. There seems to be a whiff of dead fish about all this. He's probably now working for Carmen Vlaxi.'

Pel nodded. 'What's the drill when somebody wants to build something?' he asked.

'You put in plans and an application.' Darcy said. 'They go before the Maire and the local committee. If they approve, the papers are passed on to the Sous-Préfecture. If the Sous-Préfecture approves, they go to the Préfecture and then the Conseil Général.'

'So if it's controversial there are places where it can fall by the wayside?'

'Unless sweeteners are offered. It's not unknown.'

'What happens next?'

Darcy shrugged. 'When it reaches the Conseil Général it goes through with dozens of other applications. Developments. Garages. Service stations. Alterations. Swimming pools. Additions to houses. But at that level they can't possibly know the districts so, if it has local approval, there's not much of a problem. We go for new property in a big way in France. The Government's all for it and you can get low-cost loans and tax advantages. Except for foreigners, old houses are *out*.'

*

It was suddenly all very interesting and growing more so every day, and that evening it took another step forward when Superintendent Goschen telephoned from London. 'I've got something that might be of interest to you.'

'Inform me.'

'Lloyd Jones, our half of the consortium, is, as his name suggests, Welsh. So, as it happens, in spite of his name, is Cornelius. *He* goes in for property abroad. A lot in Holland. That's why we thought he was Dutch. They seemed to be involved in a swindle which, if not international, was at least cross-border.

'He comes from Cardiff,' Goschen went on. 'And a few years ago he got into a little trouble while working for a publicity company called Bolt Marketing. Helped himself to funds and did a little time. Any interest to you?'

'Yes,' Pel said. Bolt Marketing, he remembered, had been the company which had employed Bronwen Davis in the days when she met Raby-Labassat. 'A great deal.'

'There's something else. Lloyd Jones was expecting to leave for France on the fourteenth of September. Wasn't that around the time your Baroness disappeared?'

'Yes, it was. *Did* he leave?'

'No. He was telephoned at the last minute not to.'

'Who by?'

'We don't know. He's in the States at the moment and is likely to be there for a month or two. We're told it's some development in Florida. American-British company. Our information came from his secretary. I think he's lying low.'

'Who telephoned him?'

'She didn't know. A man, she said. She didn't recognize the voice. He telephoned to tell Lloyd Jones it was all off.'

'What was all off?'

'She didn't know. But the message was that developments that had been planned might have to be altered. Lloyd Jones left the next day for the States.'

Well, it didn't indicate much but it seemed to suggest

once more, as Pel had begun to suspect, that the burning of suitable sites and the murders were somehow connected. It was too much of a coincidence that the Baroness's death had occurred on or around the day when Lloyd Jones had been warned not to appear in France.

'Daniel,' Pel said, 'let's go and see Charrieri again.'

17

The sun in Lyons was hot and reflected from the windows of Charrieri's office as if they were mirrors. Outside, lordly among the meaner vehicles of his staff scattered about the huge car-park, Charrieri's Mercedes stood, like a thorough-bred among common or garden creatures, the sun picking up the metallic silver of the paint. Inside, the stairs were still barred and the lift still out of order, the little shops empty.

Claude Dumanoir, the draughtsman, rose from his drawing board as they entered. 'He won't be long,' he said. 'He's just getting rid of a client. People get nervous when they see the cost of what they're intending to do. Or else it goes to their head and they start wanting additions they later discover they can't afford.'

'What's your job?' Darcy asked. 'Exactly.'

Dumanoir grinned again. 'I'm the one who makes His Highness's ideas look pretty and alters all the plans. The great man does the originals. Alterations are done by serfs. I also make the coffee and run errands. But not for much longer. I've got a job on *Le Bien Public*.'

'Drawing faces?'

'Caricatures. That sort of thing. You never know. I might decide not to be a second Renoir and become a Caran d'Ache instead.' Dumanoir had been scribbling in a sketch pad as he talked and he now pushed it forward. 'That's what

I want to do.'

Darcy found himself looking at a quick sketch of Pel. It was easily recognizable.

'Mind if I look?' Darcy asked, picking up the pad.

'Help yourself. If you want your wife, your children, your best girl produced as a portrait, remember me.'

Darcy turned the leaves of the sketch pad over idly. Then he stopped. In front of him was a sharp pencil portrait of Auguste Raby-Labassat.

'That's Auguste Raby-Labassat,' he said.

'Is it? I wouldn't know. I just draw them. I don't always know the names.'

'Did he come here?' Pel asked.

'If he's in there, he must have done. I don't go out of the office. I practise on people when they come in. While they're waiting. Sitting where you're sitting. The light's very good there.' Dumanoir smiled. 'I once actually sold one. It was shockingly flattering. I suppose that's why.'

'Why didn't you show us this before?'

'I didn't know you were interested.'

'What did Auguste Raby-Labassat come to see Charrieri about?'

'You'll have to ask His Highness. He doesn't take me into his confidence.'

Darcy turned more leaves and showed the sketchbook again to Pel. 'That's Jaunay,' he said. He turned to Dumanoir. 'What did he want?'

'I don't know.'

'Did the Baroness ever come with him?'

'Baroness who? I don't know any baronesses. There was certainly a woman who came once or twice.' The boy turned a few more pages of the book. 'That's her. Is she this baroness who was murdered?'

'Yes.'

'Did His Highness murder her?' Dumanoir looked as though the idea intrigued and delighted him. 'On the other hand, I think she'd have been more likely to murder *him.*'

'Why?'

'The last time she came she left in a bad temper.'

When they were shown into Charrieri's office by the pneumatic secretary, he was presiding at his drawing board as though he were planning a campaign. There were two other architects, his assistants, standing by his side, and, as Dumanoir warned, there was an aide taking notes.

The secretary tried to persuade Pel to be brief but he wasn't having any. Charrieri watched her efforts with an amused smile, then he gestured at her to desist and finally waved away his staff.

Pel produced the charred maps and the few pages of plans Brochard had rescued from the stove at Evian. 'Seen these before?' he asked.

Charrieri studied the torn, blackened and stained papers. 'Should I have?' he asked. 'They look as though the mice have been at them.'

'They were burned,' Pel said coldly. He decided he didn't like Charrieri much.

Charrieri shrugged. 'I'm sorry, Chief Inspector, but I've never seen them before.'

Pel fingered a plan which was spread out on Charrieri's desk, held down by glass paperweights at the corners. 'They seem to be on the same sort of paper as this,' he commented.

'Not surprised.' The shrug came again. 'All architects use it. It's common to all planning offices. Are there fingerprints on it?'

Pel didn't answer because he knew there weren't. The rough handling the papers had had, the soaking and the burning, had removed all traces.

'Could they have been done in this office?'

'Not without my knowledge. You could ask Dumanoir. He touts around for odd jobs.'

'This doesn't look to me like an odd job,' Pel said. 'Do you ever work from home?'

183

'Never. When I go home all I want to do is relax.'

'Many architects put their thoughts on paper at home.'

'Not this one. Ask my wife.'

Pel paused, staring at the floor. 'Why did Baroness Raby-Labassat come to see you?'

'About the gymnasium. I told you.'

'Then why did she leave the last time in a bad temper?'

Charrieri tried to explain. 'She wasn't satisfied with the plans I'd drawn up.'

'Why not?'

'I don't know. I said they'd still have to be paid for and if she wanted more she'd have to pay for those, too. I was growing bored with her.'

'Why did Jaunay come to see you?'

'He was often in here. We did plans for him once or twice. Nothing big. He wasn't that kind of builder. He'd have liked to be but he didn't have that sort of capital.'

'And Auguste Raby-Labassat? Why did he come to see you?'

Charrieri gave a high-pitched laugh. '*Mon Dieu*, Chief Inspector, you know what I do every minute of the day.'

'I'm interested in why Auguste came to see you.'

Charrieri sat at his desk, his hands together in the form of a steeple. He thought for a moment, then looked at Pel. 'He wanted to know something about costing,' he said.

'Costing what?'

'The chateau.'

'What was he thinking of doing?'

'He was hoping, he said, to put in central heating. But he wanted to do it in a way that wouldn't harm the interior.'

'What would it cost?'

Charrieri laughed again. It put Pel off. He didn't like people who laughed too much. 'A fortune. It was just wild dreams. I knew he hadn't enough funds. And, though he was in here for an hour arguing, I didn't send him a bill for wasting my time. Normally I'd charge for such a consultation. But because of the Baroness's death I didn't. He'd already had a shock when I told him the cost. He'd have had another if he'd seen the sort of bill I would normally have sent him. My fees are pretty high – even for a consultation.'

'What did he decide?'

'Nothing. I told him central heating in that place would destroy it. It's had no heating since it was built at the beginning of the last century. Nothing would fit after one winter of heat. It would finish it off,' Charrieri shrugged, '– if it isn't already finished. They should have done something about it fifty – eighty – years ago. Central heating wasn't unknown then. It's too late now. All they can do now is let it fall down. And it will, in its own good time. The only thing they could do is tear all the inside out except the stone staircase and start again. The retaining walls are sound.'

'Did the Baroness ever come with a man called Gilliam?'

Charrieri gave the matter some thought. 'Yes, she did. He was an artist, she said. He was a friend of hers. I suspected at the time he was a bit more than that.'

As they climbed into the car, Darcy looked at Pel.

'Gilliam,' Pel said thoughtfully. 'Let's call and see him.'

They heard loud voices coming from Gilliam's house as they arrived and Darcy discreetly parked the car a few yards away along the street. Gilliam's wife appeared. She was clearly still very angry. She climbed into her car and shot off down the hill in the direction of the city.

'She seems to do that a lot,' Pel observed.

'No wonder he paints,' Darcy said.

Gilliam was busy over a water-colour of a field of sunflowers with a deep blue sky and green hills in the background, with a church steeple and a group of houses in the foreground framed by a pair of eucalyptus trees. He seemed unmoved by his wife's departure.

'Nice picture,' Pel commented.

Gilliam smiled. 'Straightforward pictorial,' he said. 'Not very imaginative. But very popular. I can do them with my eyes shut. I had a lot of practice. I used to paint pretty water-colours for estate agents' windows.'

'As an architect?'

'Not really. I was very young. I wanted to learn to draw buildings and I considered that a year or two in an architect's office would help. My family wouldn't be seen dead drawing plans for other people — except for city halls, cathedrals and that sort of thing.'

'Did you draw plans?'

'Copied. Copying plans was part of the job. I didn't stay long. I went into the army. My eldest brother was running the estate. My other brother went into politics. I decided on the army. They used me to draw plans for new barrack plumbing.'

18

Misset was all smiles when he appeared in Pel's office.

Pel regarded him coldly. He had just arrived from Gilliam's and he was puzzled. He felt he had the solution to all their mysteries hovering at the back of his mind but somehow it just didn't fit.

'Well?' he snapped.

Misset's smile grew wider. He had been conducting an enquiry as ordered but he had kept it low-key and leisurely. It hadn't even been hard to find what he wanted. Tar-le-Petit wasn't a very big place and, like most villages, its inhabitants talked — usually too much and usually about other people's business. He had found that Clos had been living in one of the barns of the devastated farm.

'He was camping out, *patron*,' he said.

'And Feray?'

'I think he meets his wife somewhere. I've been trying to find out where. I'm still looking.'

Pel glared. 'You stupid idiot,' he snorted. 'Clos and Feray have been in custody for days!'

Misset's jaw fell. 'I hadn't heard, *patron*. Here?'

'Evian. Same charge they'd have faced for Tar. Vandalism and a few others. Attempted murder, for instance. Theft of a boat. Assaulting a police officer. That's all we can make it at the moment. Surely to God you read the reports?'

Misset searched his mind for something that might

redeem him. 'I heard that Feray had been back at Tar,' he said.

'Not lately, he hasn't.'

'No, *patron*. Not lately. A few weeks ago. I showed that picture around that we had of that type, Espagne. I thought he might have been involved there. Two people recognized him. I think he's in with Clos and Feray.'

'I *know* he is! Sometimes you show a glimmering of sense. It's usually a mistake but it happens.'

'Did they do the job, *patron*?'

'I'm sure they did. It's well within the boundaries of their capabilities. Burn it or bash it. It's all the same. What else?'

'Well, I once saw Feray in the city here. I remember now.'

'When?'

'It was just before we started looking for him. I knew him. I once pulled him in for assault, you'll remember. I was in the Palais des Ducs paying some bill or other. He was with this guy in the hall — talking.'

'An official?'

'I think he is, *patron*. I think he works for the Conseil Général. Highways Department or something. There was another type with them.'

'Who?'

Misset had a feeling he'd failed again. 'I didn't see that one exactly,' he said. 'He had his back to me. But I'm sure I knew him.'

'How?'

'By his voice.'

'By his voice? With his back to you?' Pel snorted. '*That* would stand up well in court.'

As Misset left, Lagé appeared, his arms full of papers.

'There's a company here, *patron*,' he said worriedly. 'It's called Barbi Enterprises. It's supposed to be a construction promotion company. I gather it opened an office in Evian and

188

promptly closed it again a month later. I think it was a sort of clearing house.'

'There seem to be a lot of strange firms mushrooming up lately,' Pel growled. 'I've already come across around five. Did the owners of the office know who operated it?'

'No. It was rented through an estate agent. I gather it was a group who were putting up money for building and needed a headquarters. I was told they were interested in land at Tar.'

'Recently?'

'Some time ago. It sounds fishy to me.'

'It does to me, too. Go on. There's more?'

'Yes. The names they gave all seemed to be phoney but one of them was heard to mention a telephone number in Lyons. The estate agent was a bit suspicious and made enquiries. It was a firm of solicitors.'

'Name?'

'Paillat, Hégrion and Michel. I gather they're noted for looking after shady characters.'

'Anything on them?'

'Nothing, *patron*. But wasn't the name, Michel, mentioned in connection with some other affair?'

It was indeed.

Pel spent the night worrying.

When Lagé had gone, he'd spent some time staring at his desk. If Clos and Feray, who'd been at Tar and at Evian, knew people in the offices of the Conseil Général, then there must be others who were in the fiddle, too.

'When he'd reached home, Yves Pasquier from next door was seated at the kitchen table tracing what looked like the plan of a fortress.

'He's doing his homework,' Madame Pel explained. 'They've had to go out next door and they asked us to keep an eye on him for an hour.'

189

'I can keep an eye on myself,' Yves Pasquier said. 'I'm old enough.'

'You never know,' Pel observed. 'There may be gangsters hiding in the drive waiting to waylay you. Would you like to borrow my gun? What are you doing?'

Yves looked up and grinned. 'History. I'm tracing one of Vauban's fortresses.'

'Sebastian le Prestre de Vauban.' Pel nodded approvingly. 'A good Burgundian. Expert at sieges and master-builder of fortifications. Which one is that?'

'Strasbourg. I've also got to do Lille. I'm supposed to copy it carefully but if you rub pencil on the back and then go over the lines with a hard pencil it comes out on the paper underneath.'

Pel inspected the table top. 'It also comes out on the table top,' he commented. 'Indented into the wood.'

For some reason the incident had stuck in his mind and he lay awake half the night thinking about it.

In his office the following morning he sat at his desk frowning. His mind returned to Yves Pasquier's homework.

He was about to take out a cigarette when he realized he was already smoking one. Disgusted with himself, he thrust the packet away and, taking the cigarette he was smoking from his mouth, pinched out the end. After all, you couldn't waste good cigarettes. Relax, he told himself. Think of something else. Forget cigarettes. Unfortunately, after two or three minutes of deep thought, he came to the conclusion that the only thing he could think of was the cigarette he so desperately needed. Returning to the one he had pinched out, he stuck it in his mouth and relit it. After the first drag, he sat up. 'Of course,' he said out loud. 'Of course.'

He was remembering his talk with the Baron de Mougy. It had concerned the Raby-Labassats' sad lack of judgement where money was concerned and their vain hope of hiding their investments. 'They thought the government didn't know,' De Mougy had said. 'But they always find out. There are ways of finding out.'

Indeed there were.

There was a plan. Jaunay had said there was. And if there were, someone somewhere had seen it. De Mougy was right. It was something they had all overlooked. Planning permission. Bureaucracy's brevet. Officialdom's OK. The management's concordat. It *had* to be in the records. If it weren't, something was wrong.

Leaning across the desk, he searched among the papers spread there for the telephone. He found it by hauling on the cord. As it emerged from under the papers, he lifted the handset. 'Get me the City Archives,' he said.

He was on the telephone a long time. When he'd finished, he rang his wife at her office and suggested lunch. He then replaced the telephone and headed for the office of the regional architect, an old friend of his.

The regional architect studied the papers Pel laid on his desk and frowned. 'Where did these come from?' he asked.

Pel explained.

'They should never have been passed.'

'I suspect they might have been, all the same.'

The regional architect stared at the plans again and frowned, then he switched his attention to a large-scale map alongside him. 'This road here's supposed to be still secret. It was mooted and abandoned and only came up again six months ago. The plan's supposed to have been seen only by heads of departments.'

From the regional architect's office, Pel headed for the Highways Department. The director was a small fussy man Pel had also known for years. He explained what the regional architect had said.

'Why is the road being moved?' he asked.

The director told him.

'Who would know about it?'

'Me. The regional architect and one or two others. We don't shove this sort of thing around for people to see.

People have been known to go in for a bit of speculation.'

From the Highways Department, Pel went to the Water Board. The director looked at him with some suspicion.

'Where did you get this information?' he asked sharply.

'I asked a few questions and got a few answers,' Pel said.

'Who from? This information made public could bring up a whole lot of protests. From the Green lot. Land preservation societies. That sort.'

'The river's being re-routed, isn't it?'

'Yes.'

'I've heard nothing of it.'

'Well, you wouldn't, would you? It's not been announced yet.'

'Why is it being re-routed?'

'The government's given permission for a dam at Calotte-Montrachel. It's a good area for dams round there. It's a fast-flowing river, the valleys are deep and the hills are high. It's not a big dam — it's not the Aswan — but they're going to drown a village.'

'Faux-Villecerf?'

'Good God, no! Faux-Villecerf's too high. It's Taillude. There are several streams there and it's planned to build the dam on the Tarine and direct the other streams into the Ouronne to act as the spillway. It's to protect the riverside villages downstream. There've been one or two disastrous floods down there in the past.'

Pel was listening with a deep frown. The director was clearly not very happy about the project.

'The consortium who got the contract claim they're going to evaluate the wild life and protect the environment. But they're already being called "The Assassins of the Tarine". Taillude's a poor area but further downstream the Tarine flows back into the mainstream north of Lyons, and there's industry there, and big houses owned by wealthy people. There's a lot of influence.'

'Why doesn't anybody know about it?'

'Policy. People will protest. I'm protesting. There's also a society called "The Friends of the Tarine". Nature conservationists. Greens. That sort. People who want to protect the environment. After all, we don't do much about that sort of thing in France. I'm behind them on the quiet. The government daren't let it out of the bag yet because of the fuss that's being made over the proposed damming of the Upper Loire. But it'll have to come out in the end.'

Pel stared intently at him. 'I think it's come out already,' he said. 'What about the Ouronne? What will happen to that?'

'It'll become wider. Very wide, in fact. It'll cover the meadows alongside for fifty kilometres. Anything up to ten to fifteen metres deep in parts. The people who're building the dam are talking of making use of it. As a lake. For sail-boarding. There'll be a restaurant and beaches. It would recoup some of the cost of the dam. It would also be a sop to local protests. But it would also bring a flood of applications for building. People like water frontage.'

Pel was silent for a moment. 'Who else would be likely to know of these plans in addition to you?' he asked.

19

Leaving the Water Board, Pel picked up his wife and they lunched at their favourite restaurant, the Relais Saint-Armand. Despite his outward manner, Pel was a sentimentalist at heart and it was at the Relais Saint-Armand that he had first met Madame. It hadn't been a romantic meeting. Pel had been going through a period of trying to roll his own cigarettes in an effort to cut down smoking and he had been struggling with one when Madame, on the next table, had found her interest caught. She had watched him light it and watched it disappear in a puff of smoke and a shower of sparks. 'Do you ever set yourself on fire?' she had asked and they had continued from there.

He was trying to explain his problems over the Raby-Labassat case. 'It just doesn't fit,' he said. 'It ought to but it doesn't. The Planners would never allow it.'

With her business background, Madame was wise in the ways of officials. 'Like everybody else,' she pointed out, 'planners are far from perfect. They make mistakes. Sometimes they're even greedy. So are bankers. The manager of the bank at St-Frond, a man called Coubertin, handled my Aunt Violette's estate for years and when she died I found he'd managed to get her house made over to him.'

'What happened?'

Madame smiled. 'I had a better banker and he got it

overturned. Coubertin retired rather suddenly and went into business as adviser to a company that constructs golf courses. He plays a lot of golf.'

Escorting his wife back to her office, Pel headed for the Planning Department. It seemed as difficult to see the man at the top as it was to see the President of the Republic. He obviously believed in his own importance and liked it to show.

The waiting-room was as big as a football field. At one end was a door with a large plaque on it, *Hugo Lorrière, Director of Planning*, and alongside it a large notice in red which stated peremptorily NO SMOKING. Non-smokers, Pel decided sourly, were making it so difficult, smokers would soon have to have dives like opium dens.

When he asked to see Lorrière, he was handed a form on which was printed *Name? Address? Business?* He glared at the receptionist, a stiff-faced woman with blue hair and a perfume strong enough to make his knees buckle.

'What's this for?' he demanded.

'You can't get in to see Monsieur Lorrière unless you fill it in,' she said sharply. 'He's a busy man.'

Pel filled in the form with savage pleasure.

Name: Pel. Chief Inspector, Brigade Criminelle, Police Judiciaire.
Address: Hôtel de Police.
Business: Murder.

This last he crossed out and replaced with *Double Murder*. Underneath he added a line of his own, *Time of appointment*: and answered it with *Now*, which he underlined twice and then, for good measure, added three exclamation marks.

The blue-haired woman picked up the sheet languidly as he skated it across the desk to her but as she read what had been written her eyebrows shot up as if she were a terrorist who'd suddenly discovered she was sitting on her own

195

bomb. In no time at all two or three people were running round in a hurry. It seemed Monsieur Lorrière had been taking a calm afternoon tea with his subordinates and Pel saw two plump young men hurry out of his office, carrying cups and saucers.

Lorrière's office matched the rest of the department and looked as though it contained a few additions supplied by Lorrière himself for his comfort. The walls were covered with framed photographs from which it was clear that, like Madame's banker, Lorrière was a golfer. He came forward to meet Pel. He was a large handsome man, always something to put off Pel, who was neither, and he wore the eager smile of a man about to meet his mistress.

Pel ignored the smile. 'I see you enjoy a game of golf,' he said.

'Yes.' Lorrière was clearly trying to establish himself as a man full of the milk of human kindness. But there seemed to be an edge of nervousness beneath his smiles.

Pel indicated one of the photographs that had caught his attention. It showed Lorrière holding a silver trophy. Alongside him was another man holding a putter. On either side was a woman. 'You seem to win things,' he said.

'Final of the Malmort Members' Foursome,' Lorrière said. 'That's me and my partner, Dugusse, the lawyer. I expect as a policeman you've come across him in the Palais de Justice now and again.'

'Yes,' Pel agreed. 'Now and again.'

'With our wives,' Lorrière said. 'They wanted to be in the picture. They usually do, don't they?'

'Usually,' Pel said. His smile looked as if it had been hired for the occasion.

'Amazing how golf's caught on in France.'

'Amazing. My wife's bank manager was a great golfer. Your class of player, I imagine. Name of Coubertin.'

Lorrière's face went blank, as though he had walked away and left the smile behind. 'I've met him,' he said. 'Played with him once on holiday. On one of those courses they have in Portugal. They build a lot down there. Money in them. As a banker, he was interested in the developments. What can I do for you?'

Pel's mild manner changed abruptly as he slammed down the file he was carrying and opened it to show the plans he had brought. 'Ready to go to the Conseil Général for approval,' he pointed out. 'I gather they've been improperly presented.'

Lorrière peered at the plans, his face suddenly grey.

'How did they come to be passed?' Pel persisted.

Lorrière looked uncertain. 'I — I can't imagine.'

'Why wasn't it noticed?'

'You can't expect us to examine everything in detail.'

'Isn't that what you're here for?'

It gave Pel a great deal of pleasure to provide Lorrière with an unhappy half hour. 'Were they presented to the Planning Committee?'

'I suppose they must have been.'

'Must they indeed?' Pel eyed Lorrière coldly. 'Who else would see them? Besides you.'

It seemed to be time to see the Prefect. He was a big man like the Chief who took his duties seriously. Maires and minor officials existed to do what the people wanted. The Prefect had been appointed by Central Government to see that they didn't get away with it.

Pel tried him first on the subject of foreign house buyers.

The Prefect frowned. It was obviously a subject he didn't enjoy discussing and he made a little speech on the subject.

'It's a problem,' he admitted. 'We want to develop these poorer backward areas, and allowing people to build is a way to do it. Some of rural France is a backwater and should be opened up. We're even making grants to do it. But people in rural areas don't want it opened up. They consider it's

197

their land and resent the intrusion of foreigners. They feel unbridled development could fill the village streets with GB cars. It's a question that splits whole communities and brings bitterness.'

He was trying to see all the angles to the question at the same time. It was difficult to tell whose side he was on and so far he wasn't saying. On the other hand, the merest whiff of stinking fish was enough to put him on the alert.

He sat up at Pel's query, obviously startled that Pel knew about it. His response was exactly the same as the director of the Water Board's and Pel answered it in the same way.

'Where did you hear about that?'

'I asked a few questions and got a few answers.'

'Nobody's supposed to know about that.'

'Then it's time they did. Is it going to come off?'

The Prefect decided it was time to climb down from the fence. 'I think it will,' he said. 'It's a Paris project and Branco Construction's powerful enough to pull a few strings.'

Branco Construction, Pel remembered, was the firm which had wanted to build on the shores of Lac Léman and had been refused permission. Doubtless, they'd find the people behind Branco were the same faceless people who were involved with the plans for other places that had turned up.

'Of course,' the Prefect pointed out, 'if there's any suggestion of influence being brought to bear, the whole thing could fall through. And there might be. People have certainly been approached. One or two who were against the dam at first have suddenly switched sides. Perhaps somebody's been persuading them. Branco have a lot of money to throw around.'

'What's your position, Monsieur le Préfet?'

The Prefect frowned. 'I've spoken against it. It could cost me my job.'

'When is it likely to be finished?'

'They've estimated three years. Why? What's this all

about? Is somebody dipping their fingers into it?'

'It begins to look like it.'

'It could kill it dead. Are you on the case?'

'I'm investigating a murder. Two murders, in fact.'

'The Raby-Labassat case?'

'Yes.'

'Do you think they're connected with the building of the dam?'

'I do now.'

The Prefect suddenly smiled. 'You'd better clear it up,' he said. 'I hear there's panic among the British residents.'

'Why? What's the difference between British murders and French murders?'

The Prefect's smile became a grin. 'Perhaps,' he suggested, 'ours are bloodier.'

When Pel returned to his office there was a message waiting for him to ring Chief Lapeur of the Fire Brigade. Instead of telephoning, he got into his car and went round to Fire Brigade Headquarters. Chief Lapeur had a list for him, of fires he considered might have been deliberately set alight. There were more than Pel imagined.

'Where did you get these?'

'From Records. You'd be surprised how many people are in danger of ending their days as a heap of ashes. In spite of fire warnings and ceiling sprinklers. Have *you* got an alarm?'

Pel hadn't and he was startled enough to decide to get one.

Chief Lapeur produced a couple of bottles of beer and went off on to his favourite subject – fire, and what caused it. He delivered a long diatribe about mistakes that were made and ended with, 'You'd be surprised how many buildings could go up in smoke tomorrow.'

Returning to his office, Pel sat for a while, deep in thought, then he telephoned Cousin Roger. Cousin Roger sounded

199

as if he'd had a good lunch with a lot of wine.

'Are you well in around there?' Pel asked.

'Well in? What do you mean?'

'Do people know you?'

'Very well. They cross the road when they see me coming.' Cousin Roger laughed. 'Of course people know me.'

'Everybody? Estate agents, for instance?'

'We back one.'

'Bank managers? Fire chiefs? Insurance brokers?'

There was a puzzled silence and Pel went on. 'I have a few questions I want answering.'

'Do I get paid?' Roger asked.

'No.'

Roger's sigh was audible. 'I didn't think I would be,' he said. 'Fire away.'

Pel told him what he wanted and he could hear papers being shuffled. 'That all?'

'No. There's some more. Know an accountant by the name of Tussot?'

'Very well. Lives at St-Frond. Plays a lot of golf.'

'What do you know about him?'

Roger paused. 'Well, since we're on the telephone, I'll just say I prefer not to do business with him.'

'Is he a crook?'

'You said it, not me.'

'How about a banker called Coubertin?'

Roger laughed. 'He's the type who tried to diddle Aunt Violette out of her house. He had ambitions to be a tycoon and rule the world. *He* comes from St-Frond, too.'

'Yes, he does. Do they know each other?'

'Like goes to like. I shouldn't be surprised.'

'Know Dugusse, the lawyer?'

'What is this? Some sort of thieves' kitchen you've dug up. Yes, I know Dugusse.'

'He used to be Maurice Tagliatti's lawyer. You'll

200

remember Maurice Tagliatti. I think he's Carmen Vlaxi's lawyer now.'

'Is he indeed?'

'Does he know this Coubertin and your friend, Tussot?'

'I dare bet he does. I'll check.'

Cousin Roger rang back that evening. 'They know each other,' he said. 'Same golf clubs. I'll let you know the answers to the rest of your questions shortly. They're not so easy.'

The following morning, Pel put his head in the sergeants' room. It had all the ease and comfort of the hold of a ship. The floor was covered with cigarette ends – cops were always the last to get worked up about not smoking – the waste baskets were all full, and it had a stale atmosphere that came from nobody ever bothering to open a window. Nosjean was writing his report on the Genois garage case. He was pecking at a typewriter – slowly, because he only used two fingers and, like all the typewriters in the sergeants' room, the one he was using was a reject from the typing pool. The rejects from the typing pool always landed in the sergeants' room. On the wall above his head was a notice, SAVE PAPER. Under it someone had written with a felt pen, *Re-use trees*.

'Busy?' Pel asked.

'The usual, *patron*. Up to the eyeballs.'

'Good. You'll have plenty of time then. I want you to do a bit of checking for me. Fast.' Pel handed a list of names across the desk and his finger jabbed. 'Dugusse,' he said. 'What do you know of him?'

'Only what's in the files, *patron*. He's careful to keep his nose clean. Doesn't get involved. But that doesn't mean he's straight.'

'Find out more about him, will you?'

'What are we after?'

'Whom he knows. What he does. I believe he plays golf, for instance. At Malmort. Find out who he plays with, drinks with, eats with, spends his weekends with.' Pel's finger rested on the list of names. 'What this lot are doing.'

'That's a lot of names, *patron*.'

'What's De Troq' up to?'

De Troq' had already signed off, leaving the details to Nosjean. Nosjean assumed he was with the girl from the Palais de Justice, whose family also had a title. De Troq' wasn't a snob but he liked to move in the right society.

'Call him in,' Pel said. 'I want to know all about the people on that list. Whom they know. What connection they have with each other. What they're up to. And quickly. Get on with it.'

Nosjean came back forty-eight hours later. He looked tired but he had a notebook full of names. Most of them were names Pel was interested in. 'They all seemed a bit on edge,' he said.

Pel nodded. 'Well, they would be,' he agreed. 'Who's first?'

'Lorrière,' Nosjean began. 'Plays golf.'

'Who with?'

'Various people. One, an accountant called Tussot. Two, a banker called Coubertin. Three, an architect called Michel. Four, Dugusse.'

'Anyone else?'

There was a woman called Jacqueline Defay who had turned out to be a cousin of Dugusse and worked in the surveyors' office. She and her husband, who was deputy director of the Highways Department, had a weekend home on Lac Léman.

Pel's eyebrows shot up at the information.

'Evian, *patron*,' Nosjean said. 'You know Evian.'

'Yes,' Pel agreed. 'I know Evian. You go down the N6 to

202

Macon, take the motorway to Bourg and Nantua, then the road runs alongside the Swiss frontier to the lake.'

Nosjean had not only produced names, he had answered a question that had puzzled Pel for a long time. What was Bronwen Raby-Labassat's interest in Lac Léman? Now they had it. She must have met Dugusse at the Defays' house at Evian and since Dugusse was connected with Vlaxi, doubtless that was where she had met Vlaxi, and Cornelius and Lloyd Jones as well. They'd been working things out and that was doubtless how Gérard Espagne had come to be in possession of those maps and plans Brochard had rescued from the family stove. He'd been there, too, to get his orders.

A lot of things were suddenly becoming clear. Gérard Espagne hadn't been in the Parc de la Columbière with Orega and the hold-up boys to receive orders about what to do with the loot. He was there to *give* orders. He'd been involved at St-Etois and Tar-le-Petit and Orega's elaborately staged hold-up had been a diversion to keep the cops busy. They had been growing too interested and he had been set up — and still didn't realize it! If he'd got away with it, fine; his reward would have been in the loot. But he hadn't and his refusal to split on what he thought were his friends had delayed matters just enough to take the heat off until things could be adjusted.

They were all part of the same outfit.

20

It still required a few telephone calls. One of them to
Goschen in London. About people Pel was interested in. 'I
want their background,' he said. 'Their financial standing.'
He had an answer the following day.

'He's considered good,' Goschen reported. 'But he makes
very little really. He'd do better if he were in England but he
can't return. His wife's family are after him.'

'Why?'

'Money. He used some of theirs. Quite a lot, in fact.
Without permission.'

'Are *you* wanting him?'

'The family refuse to lay charges. But they'd like their
money back. I gather they were prepared to start
proceedings but he's told them he can produce the money
with interest if they'll just wait a while.'

'And will they?'

'They've agreed to.'

Putting the telephone down, Pel sat staring at it for a
while in silence, his mind working. That afternoon he called
Darcy into his office.

'That car that appeared at Faux-Villecerf,' he said.
'Renault 304, black or some dark colour that could look
black —'

'There've been a few distractions, *patron*. Claudie's on it
now.'

'Good. Take a look at this.'

On Pel's desk was a large sheet made up of xeroxed copies of plans and parts of plans pasted together. They showed what appeared to be a great house. Taking a piece of rolled-up tracing paper on which Darcy could see sharp lines drawn with a felt pen, Pel opened it and placed it on top of the xeroxed copies. As he moved it about, eventually, apart from one or two areas and places that were missing, it fitted exactly over one half of the pasted plans.

As Darcy watched, Pel produced another sheet of tracing paper. Again, except in one or two places, it fitted the other half of the xeroxed copies.

'It's the Chateau de Faux-Villecerf,' Pel said. 'Claudie put it together. The tracing's from the city archives. It was built in 1813 by Ardèche Raby-Labassat. He'd just been made up to General by Napoleon and wanted something to go with the rank. His descendants added to it from time to time to make it go with their own distinctions. The plans found their way into the archives about 1900. The xeroxes underneath are from the plans Brochard found.'

He shifted the tracings a fraction. 'There were scraps referring to building plans for Evian and other places,' he went on. 'And it was a bit confusing. Then it suddenly dawned on me that two of them looked familiar in spite of being set up on different scales. When I fitted them together they became Faux-Villecerf. They were presented to the Planning Department as two separate ventures on different dates with different titles.

'Claudie got them photographed to the exact size of the original plans and did the tracing. Apart from this bit here –' Pel's hand moved, 'and another bit here, both of which don't exist any more because they were pulled down at the beginning of the century to make way for those big stone steps outside, they're the same place. There's another piece missing which was pulled down at the end of last century. The walls that are common to both plans are the outside and

205

retaining walls. The ones that have disappeared are unimportant inner walls supporting nothing.'

Darcy frowned and tapped Brochard's fragments. 'But these seem to show a restaurant, a swimming pool.'

'A hotel, in fact. Lagé worked it out. Slow but sure. He doesn't miss much. One of them was handed in at Ville d'Erf. They're all foreigners up there. It's close to the British complex at Garnier and a hotel at Faux-Villecerf would be a great attraction. I suspect someone got his palms greased.'

Darcy still looked puzzled and Pel explained. 'It was being organized by a group led by that banker, Coubertin, and included Lorrière, Journay and Gilliam and a few others from this area, plus Tussot and Dugusse and Michel. They wanted to make the chateau into a hotel and were all set to go. The plan was put in months ago. They had it all organized — cement, bricks, tiles, timber, all old stuff from Arles so they could do it on the cheap, with plans drawn in Michel's office in Lyons. The Baron had even already obligingly moved out and Bronwen was in with them. All they had to do was tear the inside out, leaving all the bits that give it grace. Exactly as Charrieri suggested.'

'They'd never get away with it.'

'They almost *got* away with it.'

'But it shows a road here, *patron*. There isn't a road.'

'There will be. The plans are with the Highways Department at this moment. The idea's to build a loop to it so that visitors won't have to go through a grubby little village street with its regular hold-ups outside the bakery when they're loading. Village streets are to be admired, photographed with the family in the foreground, but not to be used. They have cattle dung on them. They bring flies.'

Pel paused. 'But then,' he went on, 'along comes another group. With more money and bigger hand-outs. *Their* plan was better because they had more imagination and were more ruthless. Ruthless enough to set fire to places they wanted.' He laid another set of plans down. They were

206

dated later than the first set. 'Same thing,' he said. 'But much grander. Guaranteed to kill the first plan dead in the eyes of forward-looking planners.'

'Where did you get this one?'

'The planning office.' Pel's mouth twisted in a grim smile. 'I persuaded them to let me have a copy.'

Darcy stared, his mouth open. 'This shows dwellings — chalets, split-level chalets. Designed for steep slopes.'

'The Raby-Labassat land *is* steep.'

'But this blue? It shows water.'

'There'll *be* water. The river south of Calotte-Montrachel is to be re-routed. It was planned years ago but was abandoned. It's been resurrected. There's a dam going up at Calotte.'

'What!'

'It's a government scheme. It's been agreed in Paris.'

Darcy was silent for a moment. 'It would require a lot of money, *patron*. Millions of francs.'

'I think it would be available.'

'Where from?'

'Type called David Lloyd Jones. Welsh, like Bronwen. He seems to have contacts. Another called Cornelius. Also Welsh. Carmen Vlaxi — though I expect we'll never find out about *him*. There'll be plenty of people and several finance corporations in front of him. Bronwen suddenly found herself being wooed by a much more powerful group offering much greater rewards.'

Darcy stared at the plan again. 'It shows apartments —'

'In the stables, the pump house, the outhouses. A gymnasium. Bronwen was already working that one out. Swimming pool. Chalets in the grounds. The main house would be a hotel. With small shops in the hall. It's wide enough. That huge kitchen would be a bar and restaurant. There was to be a lake with sailboarding and swimming. With the dam, the River Ouronne would widen and flood all those water meadows below Faux-Villecerf. But nothing was to be built on the cheap. This group knew the international market and they decided to go in on a big scale. It's a brand new holiday village, in fact, with everything tourists need, right alongside the existing one. But safe within the boundary walls of the chateau.'

Darcy looked awed.

'There was just one snag,' Pel continued. 'The dam will take three years. But they felt they could afford to wait for the second half of the plan – the water half. They had other projects. Bronwen had to be paid, of course – those sums of 10,000 francs. She happily abandoned the first scheme for the second and was going to present the Baron with dreams of wealth beyond imagination.'

'Did he kill her because of it?'

'He never looked like a killer to me.'

Pel sat down and lit a cigarette. 'Lloyd Jones, Cornelius, and probably Tussot and Dugusse as well, because they were in with Vlaxi, also transferred their allegiance. The rest, the small men, saw all their plans going wrong and all the money they'd invested in bribes and materials – and they must have invested quite a bit – vanishing with no hope of recouping. They weren't going to be allowed to join the new group. The big boys could manage on their own, thank you. It involved a lot of scheming and a lot of companies to create a fog.' He managed a smile. 'But you can find your way through fogs,' he ended, 'if you try hard enough.'

21

His arms full of papers, Pel went to see Judge Castéou. A long talk convinced her of his views and they went together to the Chief's office. Some of the names they had were important and required careful handling.

'Was the family in it, too?' the Chief asked.

'I doubt if two of them were — except for giving their approval to getting rid of the house and trying to persuade the Baron to sell. But they hadn't the money to invest and probably never heard of Bronwen's schemes. But, of course, when the Baron died, any increase in his fortune would profit them.'

'What about the other?'

'Auguste? He's a very different kettle of fish.'

'And the officials?'

'They're guilty as hell. I shouldn't be surprised if one or two have taken hand-outs from both groups. From the first, to get their plan to the starting post. From the second, to switch loyalties and push the new plan. There's not much doubt who'd have won in the end.'

'So why was Bronwen murdered?'

'Because she changed her mind. She was heard quarrelling in the car that night in the grounds of the chateau, remember? That's what she was talking about when she said she preferred it with water. She didn't mean whisky. She meant the new scheme. And the pretty part of it was that the people in the original scheme daren't harass her openly because they were guilty of fiddles that would come out if they had.'

The Chief was listening intently.

'They were bewildered, little fish in a pond that had suddenly grown too big for them. One of them tried to persuade her. He drove her to Vieilles Etuves to talk. But she still refused and he decided the Baron was a much better bet, more easily persuaded, and he killed her.'

Pel paused. 'I think that when Bronwen disappeared, Vlaxi, Lloyd Jones and Cornelius grew alarmed and withdrew from the scheme in a hurry. It was becoming too dangerous. That's when Lloyd Jones disappeared to the States. Cornelius seems to have transferred his interest to Tar. Vlaxi's sank out of sight. But the other lot hadn't their experience and were still hoping somehow to salvage something from the mess. Whoever did for Bronwen persuaded them that her death was a fortunate accident and that the Baron would give his consent. But the old boy was more stubborn than expected. Tempers were lost and the old man disappeared down the cellar steps. No wonder nerves began to show and they all started throwing suspicion on one another. They were prepared to go in for fraud, but they weren't prepared to go in for murder.'

The Procureur, the Public Prosecutor, was brought in with two of his men and they argued over the disclosures for a long time. The names were checked and it was decided their owners should be picked up simultaneously.

'When do you want to pick them up?'

'As soon as it can be set up.'

The Chief nodded. 'It'll take a little time. You'll need every man we can raise. It's going to hit the headlines with a bang.'

Charges were prepared. The arrangements were left to

Darcy and were laid on for early in the morning. It was decided it had been going on for too long and they couldn't afford to wait.

'Somebody might take it into his head to bolt,' Pel said.

Every man who was available, plain clothes and uniform, was gathered in the gymnasium at the Hôtel de Police to receive his orders. Other places were involved, too, and many cops who had been expecting a comfortable evening at home learned that instead they could expect a boring night of waiting and smoking while transport was assembled and link-ups were organized. The following morning would find them grey-faced, with mouths like the bottom of a parrot's cage.

Pel was in his office all night. Soon after daylight the reports began to come in. Jaunay was the first to be brought in. Lorrière followed. Then Tussot and Jacqueline Defay, who worked in the surveyor's office, and her husband, the deputy director of the Highways Department. The Chief put in an appearance soon afterwards, not knowing whether to be pleased or overwhelmed by the numbers.

'Name of God,' he said. 'This is one of the biggest corruption scandals that's hit the century. It'll take months to sort out the paperwork.'

Pel looked up. 'It's more than just a scandal,' he reminded quietly. 'It's also murder.'

More men appeared: Michel. Dugusse. Coubertin. Rooms were set aside for questioning and lawyers were dragged prematurely from their beds to represent clients and arrange bail. Passports were handed over. One after the other, the people who were involved were gathered in. None of the big names were among them – no Lloyd Jones, no Cornelius, no Vlaxi. But they hadn't expected them.

Just as Pel was breakfasting off coffee and rolls sent across to the Hôtel de Police from the Bar Transvaal, Cousin Roger phoned. He sounded sober and cheerful. 'Sorry I'm a bit late,' he said. 'Difficulties are easy. Miracles take a bit longer.'

211

They talked for a long time and Pel had just put the telephone down when Darcy rang.

'One missing, *patron*,' he barked.

'Where is he?'

'God knows. He wasn't at home. Didn't appear last night. I've had a surveillance put on the house and put out an alert to airports.'

As Pel bitterly pushed his breakfast aside, frowning heavily, Claudie appeared in the doorway.

'That car, *patron*,' she said.

Pel sat up as she continued: 'Renault 304. Black. Number 9235-QX-21. It's a hire car from Voitures Remizes. Do you want me to go and check it out?'

Before Pel could answer the telephone rang again. It was Auguste Raby-Labassat's wife.

'Do you know where my husband is?' she asked indignantly. 'He didn't come home last night. Have you got him there?'

Pel looked at Claudie as he slammed the instrument down. His face was grim. 'Let's *both* go,' he said sharply, heading for the door at speed. 'It suddenly seems urgent.'

The clerk at Remizes Hire Cars looked at the dates Claudie gave him. 'That's right,' he said. '9235-QX-21. It was collected by a kid. Student, I think.'

He pushed the book at them. The signature was that of someone called Robert de Laney. Pel frowned. They'd not come up with anybody called Robert de Laney.

'What was he like?'

'Usual. Long and thin. Spots. Specs. He's just collected it again. Same kid. Same car.'

'We need that car,' Pel said. 'There may be fingerprints on it.'

'Was it used in a robbery or something?'

'More than that. Murder. Where is it now?'

'Still out. He hired it for a week. He did last time.'

Robert de Laney lived in a flat near the University with

six other students in happy and noisy chaos.

'Sure,' he said. 'I hired it.'

'Why?'

'It wasn't for me. I was just paid to collect it. It was all done by letter. I have this little service, you see. Odd driving jobs – private jobs for old ladies who've grown nervous of traffic. That sort of thing. I put a small ad in the newspaper. It helps me get through university. I left it to be picked up.'

'Where?'

'Place de la Poste. The letter said to tape the keys under the front bumper. I did. It was returned the same way. A letter came telling me to pick it up from where I'd dropped it. The keys were where I'd left them. Taped. Inside the glove pocket was an envelope with three hundred francs for me.'

'Who picked it up?'

'I don't know. I hung around but nobody turned up. But it was gone when I went back the next morning.'

'What was the signature on the letter?'

'Haven't the foggiest. It was illegible, like a lot of signatures.'

'Have you still got the letter?'

'No. I threw it away.'

'You've no idea who it was?'

'No idea. This telephone call came. No name. Just a voice. It said there'd be a letter. There was. Next day. With the fee and a hundred francs extra in it to encourage me. I didn't argue.'

'Would you recognize the voice?'

'If I heard it again.'

As they climbed into Claudie's car, she turned her head. 'Where to, *patron*?'

'Place de la Poste.'

They circled the parking lot, driving quickly up and down the rows of stationary vehicles, and left with Claudie glancing back, puzzled. She had seen no black Renault 304, numbered 9235-QX-21. Pel offered no explanation.

'Where to now, *patron*?'

'Faux-Villecerf. And fast. Auguste Raby-Labassat's there. Doing an inventory. Remember? Looking after his interests. Counting the things he's come into on his father's death.'

Claudie drove fast.

Faux-Villecerf was silent and still in the sun when they arrived. The shutters were all closed but they were well aware they were being watched. Pel was a little concerned that he had only Claudie with him but everybody else was occupied with the mass arrests. They had radioed for a back-up team from Traffic and he was hoping they'd arrive, because there was no time to waste.

The car roared through the empty streets. Outside the baker's a van was unloading flour, and one of the big tractors towing an enormous trailer was coming down the hill so that they had to wait impatiently as it rattled past, making enough noise to wake the dead in the churchyard. As they set off again, they saw a police car approaching the village along the Halève road.

Reaching the top of the hill, they saw a small black Renault tucked among the bushes and caught the number as they passed – 9235-QX-21.

Claudie stopped the car outside the gates of the chateau and they went the rest of the way on foot. There appeared to be no sign of life, then Brochard appeared silently from near the stables. His hands were still bandaged and he seemed to be surprised to see them.

'What are you doing here?' Pel demanded sharply. 'You're supposed to be off sick.'

Brochard looked sheepish. 'I had a feeling that business at Evian was somehow connected with the murder here, *patron*. I thought I'd have a sniff around.'

He looked as though he felt Pel was going to send him packing. In fact, Pel was more than pleased to see him.

'Got your gun?'

'Yes, *patron.*'

'Can you use it?'

Brochard glanced at his hands. 'Not very well, *patron.*'

'Right, then, watch that fire escape,' Pel said, indicating the wooden staircase the Baron had built from the courtyard to his mother's room. It seemed a safe place where Brochard could be useful but wouldn't get hurt any more.

As Brochard vanished, they went inside. They could hear a radio playing. It sounded content, even self-satisfied.

'Auguste,' Pel murmured. 'Enjoying his new property.'

There was no sign of the new Baron in the hall or the great kitchen and none in the small modern kitchen across the corridor. Just Sous-Brigadier Morelot's man sitting smoking. He leapt to his feet as they appeared, trying to hide his cigarette behind him. He was very young.

'Who're you?' Pel demanded.

'Masse, sir. Julien Masse. I was told to keep an eye on Monsieur Raby-Labassat.'

'He seems to be upstairs. How do you keep an eye on someone upstairs when you're downstairs?'

Masse flushed. 'I'll go at once, sir.'

'Stand still, you damn fool,' Pel rapped. 'Things have changed. Anybody else around?'

'I've seen no one, sir.'

Pel gestured. 'Right,' he said. 'Upstairs. Have you got your gun handy?'

'Yes, sir.'

'Don't be afraid to use it. Are you a good shot?'

'Yes, sir.'

It was a good job, Pel thought, drawing his own gun, because if *he* were called on to fire he would probably shoot himself in the foot.

They could hear Auguste somewhere ahead of them in one of the rooms. Pel placed a hand on Claudie's arm.

'He must be mad,' he whispered. 'He couldn't possibly

215

hope to get away with it a third time.'

They reached the landing as he spoke. Just ahead of them a figure swung round and a gun came up. Pel gave Claudie a shove that sent her reeling, just as a bullet chipped a chunk out of the woodwork where her head had been. Masse fired twice and removed a whole patch of crumbling plaster from the wall. Pel pushed Claudie into a doorway and more shots rang out. Pel fired back. He didn't expect to hit anything and he didn't, but the old walls and doors seemed to be spraying chips of plaster and wood. The stink of cordite filled the landing.

Outside Brochard heard the sound of the shots and headed at once for the staircase. He'd read his history and knew Napoleon's maxim, 'March to the sound of the guns.' He shot up the staircase like a rocket. The door to the bedroom was locked but the Baron's carpentry had not been very sound and it burst open under his shoulder charge.

The man with the gun had turned. As he lifted the weapon again, Brochard appeared from the old Baroness's bedroom in a rush and grabbed his arms. Together they reeled against the doors leading to the balcony. The doors flew open under their weight and they staggered on to the balcony. As Pel and Claudie and Masse rushed forward, the struggling figures crashed against the balustrade and Pel saw the old stonework give way before them. For a second they teetered on the edge then, still clutching each other, they vanished from sight.

22

'Name of God!' Pel yelled as he heard the crash.

Beyond the balcony was a sheer drop to the flagstones below, but when they reached it and looked out there was no sign of either Brochard or the man he'd been clutching. Then a movement from the middle of the vast box hedge below caught Pel's eye. The hedge seemed to heave and Brochard emerged from its side.

He straightened up, shook himself, shedding twigs and leaves, and blinked a few times, then he reached into the hole in the hedge where he'd emerged and, one-handed, levered out a block of stone. Shoving it to one side, he reached into the hedge again and hauled out the man he'd been wrestling with. He seemed to have come off worst. His face was scratched and one eye was a welter of blood.

Brochard became aware of Pel above. He waved and gave him a shaky grin.

'Charrieri, *patron*,' he said. 'He landed underneath.' His face went deathly white. 'I think I've broken my wrist,' he ended.

It seemed to be Brochard's arrest again, so, as soon as reinforcements arrived, Pel sent him off in the police car with Charrieri handcuffed to a uniformed cop.

Temporary repairs had been done by a doctor from the

next village. Charrieri had a broken shoulder-blade and the tough twigs and branches of the box hedge had torn his mouth and almost gouged out an eye. He no longer seemed quite sane, but they managed to get an incoherent statement from him in between falsetto complaints about his injuries. It would do as a basis for a better one later. He named names: Jaunay, Gilliam. The Welshman, Lloyd Jones. Cornelius. They weren't important now but he confirmed that Lloyd Jones and Cornelius had been behind the vandalism and the attempt to set fire to the wood at Evian. Charrieri himself had sunk money in the first venture at Faux-Villecerf and had even drawn the plans — in Michel's office in Lyons, so that his involvement wouldn't be discovered. When Bronwen had gone back on her promise to go along with them, it had been just too much. While the big boys could stand the possibility of a loss, there were a few who couldn't. Charrieri had been one.

Pel watched the cars go. He was feeling a little smug. He even felt as if the cold he'd been expecting wasn't going to materialize after all. Then, as they climbed into the car and prepared to follow, Claudie spoke.

'You knew something was going to happen, *patron*,' she said. 'Didn't you?'

'Yes,' Pel agreed. 'I knew. The car confirmed it.'

'Which car?'

'The one in the car park in the Place de la Poste.'

'I didn't see a car.'

'I did. Charrieri's silver Mercedes. He left it there when he picked up the hire car. I'd begun to think he was in the Lorrière-Coubertin group, because he knew the walls of the chateau were sound. He told me so himself. He'd obviously examined them. Why? It could only have been for the group, and with Bronwen's permission.'

He lit a cigarette, feeling he deserved it and to hell with good health. 'He was desperate for money,' he went on. 'He's badly overstretched. I got confirmation this morning.'

Cousin Roger had done a lot of digging and his message couldn't have been clearer. 'That block of offices he maintains is the biggest white elephant in Lyons. He lost money building it and the top floors have never been occupied. I hear they're inconvenient and, under the new regulations, even considered a fire hazard. His money's disappearing hand over fist. Yet his own office is overstaffed with electronics and people. It's all show. He liked to look important. There were also one or two things that went wrong, that did him no good. One at Arles. That's where they picked up all their cheap bricks and cement and tiles. He was borrowing heavily.'

'And they were leaning on him?'

'Not just the banks. I heard he went elsewhere. Shadier people in Marseilles. Even Vlaxi, I believe. I don't suppose he knows even now that Vlaxi's behind the group that ruined him. He was in deep trouble. Faux-Villecerf was the only thing that could save him. And it might have. Within eighteen months, if they could have gone ahead with it. But when Bronwen let him down,' Pel shrugged, he was a dead duck. He must have tried to approach the Baron, to get his agreement to the scheme. With no Bronwen, they needed that and, after all, the Baron couldn't have seemed as though he would be hard to persuade with all the money that was available. But, though the Baron didn't have much time for Bronwen and her ideas, he believed in law and order and the approach must have made him suspicious. When Charrieri turned up he doubtless told him he intended going to the police. Charrieri had to shut him up. But killing the old man put Auguste in the driving seat and *he* was a much firmer character. A measure of Charrieri's state of mind was the fact that he was prepared to do away with Auguste, too.'

Pel tossed the cigarette away. 'I thought he might, mind you,' he ended. 'And when neither of them went home last night it was obvious why. Auguste was eager to make sure of his possessions. Charrieri was eager to make sure of

Auguste.'

As Claudie settled herself behind the wheel and started the engine, Pel noticed Auguste watching them from the doorway. He looked shaken. He hadn't a lot to look forward to, Pel decided as they rolled down the drive. Both carefully thought-out schemes would collapse now, and Auguste would have a furious brother and sister on his neck as soon as they discovered what had slipped through their fingers. To say nothing of a draughty house and precious little money to maintain it. He wondered how long he would manage it.

The place would probably end up after all as a nursing home. As a place for old people. Even, as Charrieri and his friends had planned, a holiday hotel for foreigners. There were always plenty of agate-eyed entrepreneurs around prepared to pick up what other people dropped.